"Commands attention as a disturbing and unsettling piece of fiction . . . Discerns in contemporary family life all the incendiary power of a bomb."

Newsday

"Powerful . . . Manages to snare the audience without seeming to do so, to sneak on the reader and grab him or her in a solid, unrelenting throat-grip . . . Moving and honest all the way through."

Houston Chronicle

"A disturbing and, despite its title, very funny first novel."

The Boston Phoenix

"[Naumoff] is bitingly honest . . . a daring writer. Just when you think you have him figured out . . . he does an about-face and something akin to poetry slips in."

Richmond Times-Dispatch

"A roller-coaster ride for the emotions. . . . It prompts, by turns, shrieks of laughter and profound sadness. . . . [He] has the courage to say things about human behavior that others would skirt with a clouded flourish of romantic drivel."

San Diego Magazine

The NIGHT of the WEEPING WOMEN

Lawrence Naumoff

IVY BOOKS • NEW YORK

Part I
THE FAMILY THAT EXPLODED

Part II
THE NIGHT
OF THE
WEEPING WOMEN

Part III
THE HOSTAGE CRISIS

Part I

The FAMILY
That EXPLODED

One

Humming a song on a Saturday morning was not the kind of aggressive act that could easily be explained in a court of law as an understandable reason for murder, but it struck Ervin Neal that he might finally have to kill his wife, or get rid of her in some way.

He sat up in his separate but equal bedroom and listened to that mindless warbling, which just went on and on.

He swung out of bed. The mattress creaked. The humming stopped and both people paused. In the pause and for a brief moment, their passage through the interminable rites of late middle-age was suspended. Each listened through the walls of the separate bedrooms and gauged the state of the other. Like old-time actors getting ready to enter the stage from opposite wings, each planned the look on the face, the set of the mouth, the cast of the eyes, the angle at which the head would be held. Each planned the complicated details of posture that would set the tone for their first face-to-face meeting of the day, so that by the quickest, most indirect glance, Ervin would know what he was in for and Margaret would know, as well, with an absolute precision, what amount of bitterness or anger had been held over from the day before.

In that moment of suspension, then, as each listened to

3

the movement of the other and each prepared to meet, the day began, two weeks before Thanksgiving, in the port city of Wilmington, North Carolina.

She left her room and he determined she was coming toward his room and he held his breath as she stopped in front of his door.

"Do you want breakfast this morning?" she asked.

"Uhhh," he moaned, unable to speak to her yet.

"Does the 'uhhh' mean yes?" she asked. "If it does, do it one more time."

"Arghhh," he bellowed and charged the door.

"Thanks," she said, and walked off as he stopped midway across the room, barefoot and lost now that the charge of death was over, just an old man with bony toes and thin, hairless ankles, and nowhere to go.

Having nowhere to go with all that hatred was hard on Ervin Neal. It left him with the taste of frustration so bad it was like chewing tinfoil with his lips wired shut. He couldn't spit it out. He couldn't swallow. He just had to live with it, and he withdrew to a spot where he could nourish his deceived and disappointed soul and where he sucked on his bitterness like a toothpick.

"I'm making waffles," she called, "and we'll eat in twenty minutes."

He put his fingers in his ears to obscure her voice and went into the bathroom and washed and shaved.

"Ready," she called. He left the room for the first time since seven-thirty the night before, since the moment she had joined him on the couch, after doing the dishes, to watch television and he had quickly left to watch it alone in his room.

He sat across from her. She served him two round waffles, swimming in syrup, and he looked up slowly, across the table, first at the fat, plastic shape of Mrs. Butterworth, and then, at the real thing herself.

"Sleep well?" she asked.

"Uh huh," he said.

"I had an awful night. After you went into your room," she began, talking fast, "I changed the channel and watched the Billy Graham special and then, like some lazy thing, I stayed right where I was and watched this whole three-hour movie about murder and sex and I dreamed about it all night."

He nodded his head and kept on chewing.

"You didn't go to bed till late, did you? I heard the TV when I woke up in the middle of the night."

"I don't remember," he said.

"You never do. You take those sleeping pills and you never remember anything. You must have fallen asleep and left it on. It was off this morning, though, wasn't it? I didn't hear it."

He nodded again.

"You must have gotten up in your sleep and turned it off. Maybe you did that when you went to the bathroom. That was around three. I looked at the clock."

He glanced at the old waffle iron and Margaret looked that way, too.

"Oh gosh," she said and jumped up. "I forgot."

She lifted the top and the waffle came with it and then dropped back onto the bottom grill when she poked it with a fork.

"I'll eat this one," she said. "I'll make you another one. You don't like it crisp, do you?"

He motioned for her to bring it on, waving his hand in the air as if he were directing traffic, come on come on come on, and she carried it to him and slid it onto his plate. He finished that waffle and his fourth sausage, pushed his chair back, took his plate with one leftover sausage to the sink, set it on top of the mixing bowl, and left the room.

Margaret continued to eat, taking little bites and sipping coffee. She took her plate to the sink and daintily picked up his leftover sausage and nibbled on it, and stared out the window.

She stared across the open space of the backyard and into the pines behind it and she drifted pleasantly away, until she felt him standing behind her.

"One hour," he said and put on his jacket and went out the back door.

They were leaving in one hour to visit Sally and Robert. She was glad for that. She wanted to see her daughter.

Sally and Robert Zilman had settled in rural Chatham County, 150 miles from Wilmington and 20 miles from Chapel Hill, where they had both gone to school. Like the children of many middle-class parents, they stayed around the college town after they graduated, taking their time deciding what next to do.

That Saturday they began cleaning the house.

"It's impossible to get this old house really clean," she said.

"It looks fine to me."

"It won't to them, though. Especially Daddy."

"Forget it," he said.

They lived in an old and ruined Victorian farmhouse on twenty-six acres of land. The house was ruined because the heirs remodeled it in the late fifties with sheetrock and linoleum tile and then ran out of money and abandoned it, eventually selling it to a timber merchant who then rented it to the crews who worked at his sawmill.

"We'll do the best we can and we just won't worry about it," Robert told her after lunch when they were halfway through cleaning. "They never actually say anything about it."

"I can tell, though."

"Let them stay in that damn camper, then," he said.

"They will. At night, anyway."

They had bought the place five years ago, when they got

married, but had not yet saved enough money to do anything with it. It hadn't cost much because no one wanted to live that far out in the middle of nowhere, but even with the cheap price, they just barely made their payments each month.

"Get the dog and cat out," she said.

"I'll go out with them," he said, "and mow the yard."

He got out the lawnmower. He started cutting the thick fescue grass. He pushed the mower a few feet then stopped, just before the engine died, and then, after it revved back up, pushed it a few more feet.

After fifteen minutes, the engine overheated and shut off and wouldn't start again. As he was pushing it back to the barn, he heard something on the driveway, which was nine hundred feet long and badly rutted, and every rain made it worse.

"They're coming," he said, running in the door.

"They can't be," she said. "They never come before three."

They looked out the window. He noticed the corncrib door swinging open. He ran to close it. Sally watched her parents' camper slowly coming down the driveway. It swayed and rocked, like a ship in high seas, like an enormous aluminum monster from a nightmare, relentlessly bearing down upon the dreamer. It went from one side of the road to the other, picking its way around the deepest ruts and potholes and scraping bottom when it had no way to get around a bad spot.

"Damnit to hell," she said.

The camper rounded the curve at the bottom of the hill and started up the last hundred feet to the house. Sally turned away. She stood for a moment. She closed her eyes. The old upright Hoover vacuum cleaner roared and vibrated beside her. She could feel it through her bare feet. She picked it up and shoved it across the room and into the closet. She kicked the door closed.

She went into the bathroom. She scrubbed furiously. She

cleaned the sink and the floor and wiped the specks off the mirror. She scrubbed the brown stain the iron pipes from the old well left in the bowl and then, taking out new towels and wash cloths, put one of the towels in her mouth and bit down on it as hard as she could and then screamed into it, a muffled distant scream that died right there in the towel.

After a moment and a deep breath, she washed her face, put on a smile and trotted out to greet her parents.

Ervin drove past the parking spot to the side of the house and then backed in. He had bought the camper soon after the young couple had bought the house because he couldn't stand to sleep in the filthy old place or even use the bathroom.

"The toilet, did you see the toilet?" he had asked his wife after the first visit. "It rocked back and forth so bad I thought it was going to fall through the floor."

As he backed the camper in, he had to watch for two maple trees and his daughter's car on one side and a ditch on the other.

"Goddamnit, sit still," he yelled at Margaret, who had twisted around when she saw Sally run out and was waving at her.

"Don't yell at me," she said.

"Then be still. I've got all I can handle right here without you jumping around."

He finally got in place. As he turned off the engine Robert came out of the house carrying a twelve-gauge extension cord. He plugged it into the outlet on the porch and carried the other end to the back of the camper.

"That's the way to do it, boy," Ervin said.

Sally ran to her mother's door and hugged her and then hugged her father. She and Robert and Margaret started in.

"Hold it a minute," Ervin called. "I need some help with this stuff."

"I'll do it," Robert said, and Sally and her mother went in.

Ervin handed out a pile of plastic tables with removable legs he had bought on sale at K Mart. He stacked them on Robert's outstretched arms.

Sally saw Robert struggle with the door and ran to help. Her father came next, carrying a large ice chest.

"Steaks tonight," he said. He put it on the counter and then handed a bag to Sally. "This is for you."

It was four pairs of pantyhose.

"They were on sale, along with those tables. I know women always need stockings," he said and opened the ice chest and pulled out a garbage bag in which he had wrapped the steaks.

"I'll just get these trimmed and some seasoning on them," he said, and went to work.

Sally and Margaret took a walk down the driveway. The dog and cat went with them. The woods on either side belonged to other people and the Zilmans had a deeded access through them. The woods were undeveloped and, except for coon, squirrel and rabbit hunters, provided a buffer of privacy and the sense of a large estate.

As they walked, Sally scrapped rocks into the ruts with her shoes. The cat scooted ahead and laid traps for the dog, leaping out with extended claws and arched back.

"It's always so good to come up here," her mother said.

"I'm always glad to have you. You know that."

"I know, but if I came as often as I wanted, you'd be sick of me."

"Of course we wouldn't, Mother. You're not any trouble at all. And you're looking great, you know. Have you changed your hair? What is it?"

"Not my hair," she said. "I've lost weight. Just a few pounds, though."

She thought about it for a few seconds, looking at herself in an imaginary mirror, and then added, "But I do look good for my age, I think. I really do," she said and fluffed her hair. "Of course, all the women in our family age well. You will too," she told Sally.

"I hope so."

"It's amazing I've held up so well."

"I know."

"It's a matter of perspective, though. And forgiveness."

"Yeah. If you can do it."

"I'm not alone, you know. I have help."

"You mean . . . ?"

"The church, of course. It's a strength. Young people don't think they need it."

"Maybe they don't."

"Everyone needs it. It just takes a hard time in your life to see it, to realize it. But that's the way of the Lord. He's there when you need him."

"I'll remember that."

"Don't mock me."

"I'm not. I promise I'm not. I understand exactly what you're saying."

"You see," she said, switching the subject but only horizontally, "your father doesn't mean half the things he says. He just can't stop himself."

"I'll say."

"He needs somebody to stop him. Lately, I've been thinking about doing that very thing."

"Don't get in trouble, Mother."

"I'm not scared of him. I'm the one person who really has his number."

"How do you like the tables?" Ervin asked when the women walked in.

"Great," Sally said. "Really great."

"They're a little low, aren't they?" Margaret asked.

"Not a bit," he said. "Not one damn bit."

"Don't start cussing, Daddy," Sally said.

"Well, she finds something wrong with everything I do."

"I do not. I was just making an observation. Anyone can see that they're lower than end tables usually are."

"See?" he said, looking at Sally. "She never lets up."

"They're fine," Sally said. "Mother may be right, but we're not trying to win any awards in this house."

"See," he said.

At four-thirty the conversation ground to a dead stop. No one could think of a thing to say. It was too early for supper. Everything was already prepared, even the tossed salad, which Ervin had mixed and brought in a large plastic container.

Robert looked at Sally. She looked back and cocked her head, as if to ask, What next? He shrugged. Ervin rustled his newspaper. Margaret shifted in her chair. She lazily swung one leg over the arm of the chair and left the other one on the floor and when Ervin looked over at the dark inside of her thighs he popped up off the couch as if he'd been ejected.

"I was just thinking of this joke I heard a fellow at the post office tell the other day," he said. Ervin was assistant superintendent for postal services.

"Two men from down South were up in New York for a visit," he began. "Early one morning they were looking out the window of one of those high-rise hotel buildings and they saw this great big open truck collecting trash.

"Now down below, these nigger men were throwing the trash in the back of that truck and one nigger man says to the other, 'Look heres, Mr. Brown, that trash gonna blow away if we don'ts do something. You climb up there and lay on top of it, you hear me?'

"So the other man climbed up there and lay down on the trash, spread-eagled like, to keep it from blowing away, and the truck drove off.

"And the two men up there looking out the hotel window watched that truck drive off and one of them says to the other,

'Look yonder at how these Yankees do up here. They have throwed away a perfectly good nigger.' "

Ervin laughed. He laughed hard. He looked around the room for a response.

"That's awful, Daddy," Sally said. "Those kinds of jokes aren't funny anymore."

"I think they are," he said.

"I don't," his wife said.

"I don't care what you think," he said.

"You've got to understand," Sally said, "that things are different now. People are sensitive to things like that, even if you don't really mean anything by it."

"A good joke is a good joke, no matter who or what it pokes fun at," he said. He walked into the kitchen and fussed with the steaks.

After supper, when the evening hit another dead spot halfway between digestion and time for bed, Sally suggested they play Scrabble, forgetting that her mother took so long to make a word the game would go to hell before it was finished.

"Great idea," her father said and they set up the game on the kitchen table. It was a small table. There was hardly room for elbows. Sally passed behind Robert on her way to get ice tea and bumped his chair. He winked without looking up. When she came back and served the tea, she reached over his shoulder and bit him on the ear.

"Ouch," he said.

"Just trying to perk the old boy up," she said and took her seat. She was ready for the evening to end and to get to bed. The game began.

" 'Yo' isn't a word, I don't think it is, anyway, Mr. Neal," Robert said twenty minutes later.

"It is too."

"Time for the dictionary," Sally said.

"Yo-ho-ho and a bottle of rum," her father said as she came back with it. "It's the first word of that."

"But not a real word," she said, showing him the place on the page where it should have been.

After Margaret had struggled through the early stages of the game making simple, short words, her rack was filled with letters and when this turn came around she was stumped.

"It's your go," Ervin said.

"I know it is. Just give me a minute."

He watched the electric clock on the wall above their old refrigerator, which they had given to Sally and Robert, and when the second hand came around again, he said, "Time's up."

"Not yet," she said, and everyone shifted into a more comfortable position. She was thinking hard. She was trying to use up as many of her letters as possible, and, for a moment there, looked as if she had something as she moved one letter off the rack toward the board. She put it back, though, and in the silence, time stopped. Faucets dripped. The dog moaned in a dream. Ervin stretched. He moved his long legs under the table. His knee fell over against Sally's. She froze. In her mind she assembled legs and feet and knees under the table, trying to determine whose it was and when she was sure it was her father's, slowly eased away and stood up.

"More tea, anyone?"

"I'll take a little," her father said while Margaret shifted more letters around and pointed to spaces on the board. Ervin reached up to his breast pocket to get a cigarette, and finding his pocket empty, remembered he had quit smoking.

"Ah well," he said, and made an elaborate pantomine of lighting a cigarette and taking a deep breath. "I'll just pretend."

"Can I help you, Mother?" Sally asked after she sat back down.

"I've got it now," she said. She put out all her letters. She spelled, starting from a "c" on the board, an l . . . i . . . t . . . o . . . r . . . u . . . s. Then she looked up.

"I'm sorry," she said. "That's the only word I could think of that would use up all of the letters."

Sally looked at the board and when she realized what her mother was trying to spell, laughed and said, "Oh my God, Mother, that's a first for family Scrabble."

Just after the words left her mouth, Ervin yelled out, while grabbing at the letters, "That's not spelled right," and he shoved them back at her and knocked the board sideways, scattering everything on it.

"Well, how is it spelled then?" she shouted back.

Ervin glared at her and when he didn't say anything, Sally offered to look it up.

"Forget it," he said. "The game's over."

Ervin, cooling off now, began to pack up the game.

"I guess I really scrambled that Scrabble," he said, and Robert beeped a little laugh, like a honk of a bicycle horn.

Ervin and Margaret went to the camper. While Ervin was in the tiny toilet closet, Margaret undressed and put on flannel pajamas and got under the covers. When he came out she watched him take two Unisom sleeping tablets and wash them down with a hit from a bottle of NyQuil.

"You're only supposed to take one," she said. "And that NyQuil will give you bad dreams."

"Shut up and leave me alone," he said, and climbed up into the loft that was the closest thing within the camper to a separate room and, in the dark, took off his clothes, got under the sheets in his underwear, and after tossing and grumbling and cursing under his breath, eventually fell into nightmarish sleep. Margaret lay still until she heard him go, and then just as she was thinking she would never get to sleep, dropped off without even knowing it.

Outside the house, the dog and the cat waited to be let in. The dog scratched lightly on the screen door and the cat paced under and around him, stroking him with his tail as he walked back and forth.

Inside the house, the rooms were dark except for a lamp

in the bedroom on a table beside the bed, and the light in the bathroom, where Robert sat with Sally, who was taking a bath.

"The thing I can't understand," he said, "is why he gets so nervous."

"It's Mother. She makes him nervous. She always has."

"Always?"

"Well, nearly as long as I can remember. Maybe not when I was young. It seems like we all got along well back then."

"I don't think it's her," he said. "I think it's you."

"Wash my back," she said.

"Maybe it is her," he said, and washed her with his hand, "but it's a damn mystery, whatever it is. I've been watching him ever since we got married and I still can't figure it out."

She dried off. She put on a white cotton gown and ran through the hall and jumped in the bed. Robert finished his bath, and he came in with the towel wrapped around his waist.

"Move over," he said. "I'm freezing."

She threw back the covers, naked from head to toe.

"Come on down," she said like the game-show host.

"I almost didn't make it," he said. "I nearly fell apart right there at the table."

"I'm glad you didn't."

"It was too much. I don't think I could have paid the old woman to do a better job on him than she did."

"Daddy's very uptight about sex."

"Do tell," he said.

"Spell me some words," she said. "So I can do better at Scrabble next time." He did. After that they laughed and carried on and then, out of the blue, she asked him, "Why do you like me?"

"Well, I just do," he said.

"But why?"

"Because you're fun. You're nice. You're smart. You're good looking. Everything."

"Then why do you love me?" she asked.

"Well, because, I guess, because of who you are."

"And who am I?"

"You're the person I know. And you're mine."

"And that's all?" she asked.

"That's a lot."

"Because you know me and because I'm yours?"

"It's what I know about you that makes me love you," he said.

"And what does it mean when you say, 'because you're mine'? What does that mean?" she asked, snuggling in his arms.

"It means that you're not anyone else's."

"Well, you know that."

"Yeah, but it means that you never have been," he said.

"I might have been married before. You might not know it. I might not have told you."

"But were you?"

"But would it make a difference?"

"I don't know."

"Would I still be yours?"

"Sure, but wait a minute. Were you?"

"Don't be silly. Of course not. I was just trying to get you to tell me what you meant."

"Why are we talking about this?" he asked.

"I was just thinking about it. In terms of my parents, you know."

"Yeah."

"Want me to turn off the light?"

"I guess so."

"Want me to do anything else?"

"Yeah."

"What?" she asked.

"This," he said, and showed her a little thing or two he'd been thinking about, and a little while later, she showed him a few things as well.

Meanwhile in the driveway of the old, dilapidated house, within the smooth aluminum skin of that frigid sideshow of married life, all of this occurred unknown but, it seemed, not unfelt, as a series of cries and jerks rocked Ervin Neal while his wife slept soundly with a faint smile on her lips. She was tucked in toward the wall on the narrow bench, like a baby sleeping in a dresser drawer, a sweet sleep where a part of her life was going well, and where hidden away, she tried to make it last, and where, in the remote, uncharted regions of her dreams, she began to plan for something different.

"Anyway, if they're not up," Ervin said, after he had changed clothes in the tiny bathroom, bumping and scraping against the sides like buried alive and trying to get out of the coffin, "I'll just wake them up." Margaret stayed in bed until he left, then washed and dressed.

Every time the portable electric heater came on in the camper, the lights in the old farmhouse dimmed.

"I wish they'd turn the damn thing off," Robert said to Sally.

They were at the table in the kitchen drinking hot tea, and Sally asked, "Does it hurt the wiring?"

"No, but it bothers me. It'll blow a fuse before it does anything bad."

Ervin opened the door and looked quickly around the kitchen.

"Good. You haven't made breakfast yet. I'm going to make you my special leftover-steak and eggs dish."

"You don't have to do that, Mr. Neal," Robert said.

"Yes I do. That's why I saved the drippings."

He went to work. Margaret came in. She had some coffee.

"I don't suppose you're going to church," she said to Sally.

"No. I guess not."

"I didn't think so. I wish you'd come home on Christmas and go to Christmas Eve services with me."

"Let's talk about it later," she said. "You'll be back up for Thanksgiving. We can decide then."

Just before they left Ervin looked at the house and shook his head.

"You know," he said, "it wouldn't take much to paint it. It sure would do a lot of good. We could give you the money for Christmas," he said.

"Thanks anyway," Robert said, "but we've been saving for it and were planning on doing it anyway."

"The offer stands," Ervin said and drove off.

"Why'd you tell him that?" Sally asked.

"I don't know. It just came out."

They sat on the porch. The porch faced east. The maple trees that had been planted around the house when it was built created a canopy of shade during the summer and now shone red as they stood full of leaves ready to drop.

"It's so quiet," Sally said. The cat was on her lap and the dog was in the yard in a sunny spot.

"It always is," Robert said, "after they leave."

"I know," she said. "It's almost like when the radio or television's been on real loud and suddenly you notice it and turn it off."

They put their feet on the rail and they rested. Next weekend they had to visit his parents. The week after that the Neals returned for Thanksgiving. After that, Christmas. A solid month of madness. They shared the quiet morning then, anticipating what lay ahead.

Two

Ervin spent a lot of time in convenience stores. He spent time in them the way a person who loved art might spend time in a museum. He strolled the aisles. He looked for new products. He looked for old products in new packages.

These stores were just right for the South, where they took the place of the neighborhood bar and served people who, brought up in that generalized Baptist world of denial and abstinence, poured in junk food as merrily as red-faced alcoholics, only the store was better, because you never knew what you were going to find on the shelves. Potato chips au gratin. Corn nuts. A Mickey Mouse ice cream bar with chocolate ears.

People like Ervin passed each other in the aisles and looked at each other and stared, waiting for the other to speak. They moved in the same way and they looked for the same thing, but, unable to ask for it, they continued on. They were travelers in the neighborhood museums of the commercial arts.

Ervin's favorite store was the Pantry, where wide aisles and bright lighting and shrink-wrapped magazines of the forbidden naked female beckoned. Even on his bad days, in his worst moments, he only paused at the rack, never for a moment letting on how much he missed the sweetness of a woman, the touch, the look, the understanding smile, the comfort of someone to talk to.

It was his favorite store partly because the clerk who worked the day shift treated him so nicely that, for a moment each day, he felt a little better.

He opened one of the glass doors and reached for a can of Gatorade, but just as his hand gripped the cold orange can, he saw a sign taped on the adjoining door advertising alcohol-free beer and he closed the door where he was and stared transfixed at the new product.

"That's great stuff," the nice clerk said.

"What? That?"

"That near-beer, or, I mean, not near-beer, but whatever they call it," she said and walked through a side door and appeared behind the racks of cold drinks where she quickly, like a machine built especially for the task, racked up a whole shelf of six-ounce orange juice bottles.

Ervin pulled out one of the cans. It had a foreign-sounding name and he read the ingredients and the rest of the label.

"I wonder if it'll make my breath smell," he said. He was on his lunch break.

"I don't think so," she said as he put the can on the counter and reached for his wallet. "There's no alcohol in it."

"I guess not," he said, and paid for it.

"Come back," she called after him and he waved and took the new beverage to his car. It was a cold day, but with the windows rolled up, the inside of the car was warm as a greenhouse. As he drank, he rested sections of the free classified shopper on the steering wheel and read all the ads, even the help wanted, when the last thing he wanted was another job.

The beer was highly carbonated and he began to burp. He let it roll, and as he felt one coming on, he worked it up and let it loose, one after another, smacking his lips at the taste and swallowing again, waiting on the next.

He slumped back in the seat of his old Dodge and continued reading. He actually felt a little drunk, loose and warm and cozy in his private little world in his car in the sun. He finished one section of the shopper and tossed it onto the floor with the empty can and put the second section against the steering wheel. He opened it, felt a bit of discomfort from gas, and leaned over toward the door to let it escape.

At the same time he leaned over, he looked up to see if anyone heard and not fifteen feet from his window and walking toward him was the new woman who had come to work at the post office.

The smell was absolutely fierce. He quickly looked away. He fiddled with his keys as if he were going to start the car and when she tapped on the window he acted as if he didn't hear her, and then looked up, surprised.

"Oh, hi," he said through the glass.

She said something. He pointed to his ear and waved his hands around as if he were deaf.

"Roll it down," she said, and made a cranking motion with her hand.

"I can't," he said, and made as if to try, and acted as though it were stuck.

Meanwhile the smell had come purely out from between his hips and the seat and filled the car like poisonous gas.

She walked around to the other side and he thought, Holy cow, what am I going to do? She tried the door and then looked at him strangely. She pulled in the air beside the door lock, lifting it and pointing at it.

"Wait a second," he said, and turned the key to accessory and the blower on, and then pointed to the mess on the floor and began to throw the cans and wrappers and old newspapers into the back seat. He swept the seat itself off with his hand, and then suddenly realized his escape. He opened his door and leaped out, and then slammed it closed so hard the old car shivered and twanged like a dropped guitar.

"The car's so messy," he said, sprinting around to her side.

"I wanted to ask if I could have a ride back. I took my car

to the shop and was going to take the bus but it doesn't come in time and then was going to take a taxi when I saw you over here.''

"Oh sure," he said, "you can have a ride."

"I'm Angie," she said.

"I remember," he said. "You started a few months ago."

"Right."

"Do you want to buy anything for break?" he asked, stalling for time.

"I don't think so," she said, and then paused, when during a lull in the traffic, she heard a whirring from his car and looked in. "Something's on in your car," she said.

"Oh," he said, and reached for the handle. "I left the blower on. I was just getting ready to leave when you tapped on the window."

He pulled on the door and it hung for a moment halfway open and then snapped, loud as a gunshot, as it cleared the spot where the hinges were bent and the door dug into the supporting post.

"Yeow," she said.

"Sorry. It always does that. Old piece of junk," he said and reached in and turned off the key, leaning over at the same time and unlocking her door.

"We better go," she said and got in. He could still smell it.

"I've got so much trash in this old car it smells like a garbage truck," he said. "I just never get around to clearing it out."

"Mine's the same way," she said, and looked for her seatbelt.

"It's, uh . . . ." he said, and searched in the crack of the seat for it, ". . . it's, uh, right here, I think," and he pulled on the silver buckle, but in pulling on it made a fist and couldn't get his hand back through.

"Never mind," she said. "It's not far," and they drove off, Ervin stiff as a brick and uncomfortable in the cold air blowing in through his window, and Angie, rather innocently riding along beside him not knowing, of course, having no way of knowing, of course, that she was the first woman in years, outside of Margaret and Sally, to be alone with him. He felt downright giddy and didn't know what to make of it.

Three

Sally and Robert visited his parents once a year. It was 120 miles to Charlotte from their house. Robert's father was a dentist. He was famous for having convinced his patients, when the high-speed drill was introduced, that they no longer needed novocaine. By convincing them of this, he cut ten minutes of chair-time from each visit. He could see nearly a third more patients. He smiled and chatted happily while he drilled the tears right out of their eyes.

"There it is," Robert said, driving up to the grand house the high-speed drill had helped pay for.

"Stately mansions," Sally said.

"What's that from?"

"A book? No. A hymn, I think. I can't remember."

They parked behind the two cars already in the garage.

"This is it," he said.

"I guess it is."

"Teeth brushed?"

"Check."

"Hair combed, all lint and stray particles removed?"

"Check."

"Then we're ready," he said and they walked down the slate walk to the back door. It was locked.

"That's strange," he said. "They were expecting us. Weren't they?"

"I think," she said. "You took care of it."

"I hope it's not the wrong day."

He rang the bell. He heard his mother's high-pitched voice. It was aimed at his father.

"You know that's the back-door bell. The front bell," she said, "goes ding-dong and the back bell goes dong-ding."

Sally moved behind Robert and pulled on his shirt, hiding but letting him know she was there.

"You're late," his mother said. "What happened?"

Robert's father patted her on the shoulder, as if to say, Calm down, calm down. She was so upset at Robert for having disappointed her in so many ways that no matter what she told herself each time she was going to see him, no matter how she and her husband planned what they would say and what they wouldn't, she just spilled it all out anyway.

"Now, now," Dr. Zilman said. "They're not too late, are you?"

"I don't think so," Robert said.

"Come in and sit down. Tell us what you two have been doing," Dr. Zilman said and led everyone into the den. While the three of them talked Mrs. Zilman watched her son, who had not been close to her since he was a teenager. She had the same feeling she had always had about him that if she could just break through to him, just shake him loose from whatever it was that had possessed him, if she could just save him from whatever it was that had turned him cold toward her, then the family could be back the way it had been when Robert and his sister were young.

"Will you stay the night?" she asked and saw her husband look away, as that was one of the questions they had decided not to ask anymore.

"No, I don't think we can," Robert said. "We've just got so much to do."

"Like what?" she asked.

"Well, I mean, Sally's got her job and I've got mine . . ."

"You don't work on Sunday, do you?"

"No, but I mean . . ."

"And what kind of job is that, anyway, for someone like you, construction work, I mean, it's just not right," she said.

"It's not construction work," he said. "It's carpentry."

"Whatever."

"There's a difference."

"It's still not a career."

"Sally's got a career," he said.

She was a graphic artist at the university in Chapel Hill. She had majored in studio art at UNC and then, after a few years to play around, married Robert and took the job.

"That's not what I mean."

"How's Reecee doing?" Robert asked about his sister.

"Beautifully," his mother said.

"She's Phi Beta Kappa already."

"And just a junior," his mother said to Sally, as if she didn't know and gave her a lemon smile.

"Four-oh average," his father said.

"She always was good with books," Robert said.

In the lull, Dr. Zilman took out a thick, old Havana cigar, lit it and began to puff. Mrs. Zilman turned on an air purifier. As Dr. Zilman puffed, billows of smoke rose in the sunlight coming through the window behind him. The smoke played in the light and drifted lazily across the room. They all watched this smoke, suspended and hypnotized and warmed for a few moments by its graceful flow and by the rhythmic puffing on the cigar.

"Phi Beta Kappa," his mother suddenly said again, as if coming out of a dream.

"Double major," his father said.

"Might go into dentistry," his mother said.

"We always thought it'd be you," his father said.

"I guess that's the way things go," Robert said and noticed his mother looking at him strangely.

"What's that?" she asked and rushed over and grabbed the neck of his sweater. "Look at that spot. What is it?"

She pulled on the material and stretched it out to see it better.

"What?" he asked, looking down like an old man with bifocals trying to see what it was.

The whole family converged on him, Sally included, knowing it would be her fault he had the spot. They offered their opinions.

"It's a burn," his father said.

"It's not," his mother said.

"It's grease," Sally said.

"Grease? What kind of grease leaves a black spot?" his mother asked.

"Automobile grease," she said.

"Oh," she said and let the material pop back.

"I got that on me this morning when I was adding some oil," he said.

"And you let him wear it looking like that?" she said to Sally and rushed out of the room and then back in again carrying a spray can of K2-r.

"I'll fix it," she said and pushed Robert's head to one side and said, "Watch it," and sprayed him like a bug, whirling the can in a circle as the white foamy spray, which smelled like burning Easy-Off, obliterated the spot.

"There," she said. "Wait awhile and then we'll brush it off with the cap." She pointed the spiked plastic top at him. "I hope it's not ruined," she said and pulled on it again.

"Let me just take it off," he said.

His mother took his sweater in the kitchen and he and Sally went upstairs to his old room, which had new furniture.

"See that roof?" he asked. "That's how I used to sneak out."

"You jumped from there?" Sally asked.

"I was tougher then."

"And had more to run away from, too."

"That's right, baby," he said and pulled her down on the bed.

"Don't."

"Why not?"

"They might come in."

"Let them."

They went down for a late lunch his mother had prepared while waiting for the spot remover to work, but before she served them, she guided Robert into the other room.

"I just want to ask you one thing."

Here it comes, he thought.

"What's that?"

"I told myself I wasn't going to worry about it this year, but I have to know. I just have to."

"The answer is no."

"No to what?" she asked.

"To what you're going to ask me."

"How do you know what it is?" she asked, truly dumbfounded.

"Because you ask me every year."

"Ask you what? Go on and tell me if you're so sure?"

"If I went to Yom Kippur services this year. Right?"

"That is right," she said. "But I never remember asking you. Never. I worry about it, but I never remember asking you."

"He started to go," Sally said and Mrs. Zilman spun around to see her leaning in the doorway. "He talked about it, anyway," she said.

"I did talk about it," he said. "But I didn't make it."

His mother went out the other door to the room and circled back to the kitchen and started serving lunch.

When Robert had told them he was marrying Sally, and even after they met her, his mother had said, "Well, if you do that, you're finished. You'll be sorry for the rest of your life."

She had a low opinion of the Christian world, based mainly

on an undefined sense of competition and a two-week vacation she had spent as a college student with one of her Christian friends, which she never got over and whose faults she ascribed to everyone outside of her faith she ever fell out with.

"They don't live like we do," she had told Robert. "All you'll hear is Jesus, Jesus, Jesus from her family for the rest of your life. They keep dirty houses. Your father tells me they have bad teeth. They run around on each other. They hold the liquor bottle in one hand and the Bible in the other."

So far, Robert had found none of that to be true.

The children left immediately after lunch.

"We've got to get home before dark," he said. "I think one of my headlights is burned out."

The only thing that was really burned out was the relationship, and as far as Robert was concerned, there was no fixing it and he hadn't worried about it in so long the visit once a year was more or less on the same level as paying taxes.

"Well," he said, as they drove up Interstate 85, "one weekend I get to see your parents fight it out on a Scrabble board and the next weekend I get this."

"It's all my fault, of course," Sally said.

"Some trip," he said.

"Promise me something."

"Anything, baby," he said.

"Promise me if we ever get that bad, we'll just go our separate ways."

"Promise me something, too."

"Okay."

"Promise me if I ever get like your father you'll shoot me."

"I can't promise that," she said.

"Well I'll shoot myself, then."

"It's strange," she said, and put her feet on the dash.

"When you think about people being married, you think about people being in love. But then, what happens?"

"Beats me."

"Wonder why people stay together when everything's gone sour."

"My parents love each other," he said.

"Oh, I guess they do. It's mine I'm talking about."

"I don't know."

"I'm glad we have what we have," she said, and leaned over and kissed his cheek. "It's the most precious thing in the world to me," she said, and looked down the road ready to get back home and get on with her life, and to get past Thanksgiving, Christmas and New Year's.

They drove up to the old house just as the sun was setting. It looked good in subdued light, but with the trees losing their leaves, it looked much worse during the day as the sun illuminated the peeling paint and rotten underboxing and patched clapboards.

"I know," she said. "Let's get the house painted before Mother and Daddy come up for Thanksgiving."

"How can we do that?"

"We just do it."

"Have we got the money?"

"Barely. Maybe."

"But what about the payment?"

"We've got enough for that, too."

"I hate painting. I hate scraping. Have you ever done it?"

"I did ours with Daddy when I was younger."

"Your house is brick."

"It has siding halfway up around the windows and along the back, remember?"

"Oh yeah."

"I'm determined to do it," she said.

"I can tell."

"I'll do anything to get it done before they get here."

Four

That Sunday morning Ervin was dragged from his drug-induced sleep by the sound of organ music and choir singing. The hymn was upbeat. It was the opening theme song to a praise-the-Lord-and-pass-the-money show that Margaret watched while getting ready to go to church, where the entertainment, while not as slick as television, was good enough.

Because Margaret was going to church, Ervin wasn't. That left the whole morning to kill before the "NFL Today" program and, if things were in his favor, six to seven hours of nonstop action.

"Have a good rest while I'm gone," Margaret called to him when she heard the car horn. She didn't drive, and hadn't for years. Ervin came out when he heard her drive off.

"Good rest, my ass," he mumbled at the departing car. He flipped across the channels and paused for a moment on the East Carolina coach's show, and then turned it off and dressed.

Margaret assumed he stayed home and rested and made the most of being alone. He never did. He always went somewhere, but finding interesting places to go on Sunday morning in the coastal plains of eastern North Carolina where everything was shut up tight took ingenuity and creativity.

One of the places he often went was a hardware store in a rural community about sixteen miles from town. It was open 365 days a year, from morning until night, and sold guns and ammunition along with hardware, soft drinks, crackers and groceries.

He wandered around in the store. He knew a few of the regulars by sight, enough to nod and establish that he meant no harm, this stranger to the community. He stopped this morning in front of the gun racks. Rifles and pistols were displayed behind a locked, glass-paneled door and, within, were locked once more through their trigger guards with a chain. He bought a small Coke and a pack of Lance salted peanuts and, while he stood there, he dumped the peanuts in the Coke and then sipped on the bottle, first letting a little of the drink slide in and then opening up for a mouthful of nuts.

When he finished, he went to the hardware section and bought a tiny grease gun and a tube of grease, intent on silencing his car door. He checked his watch and then left the store in time to get home before Margaret. On the way, his car died suddenly, as if the impulse to the spark, and the gas as well, had simultaneously shut off. It didn't sputter. It didn't fire again, and he coasted to a stop in a dirt parking lot in front of a closed restaurant surrounded by fields of blueberry bushes as far as the eye could see.

He stood beside his car with the hood up and soon caught a ride into town, and then took a taxi to his house, where he saw Margaret at the window.

"My car broke down."

"But where were you? I didn't know you were going anywhere."

"I just went out for a ride in the country."

"To see who? To see what?"

"Just a ride. Just killing time. Don't worry about it."

"You better not be up to anything," she said, trying to see through him.

"Forget it," he said. "We've got to get the car."

"What do you mean?"

"Ride out with me in the camper and I'll take a chain and pull it back to Wart's garage. He can work on it Monday."

"I can't drive."

"Just steer it. You can do that. A child could do it."

"I can't. Call a wrecker."

"Cost too much," he said and handed her her coat and started out the door.

"Let me change clothes."

"No time. Something might happen to the car. It's sitting in the middle of nowhere."

"I might get dirty."

"Listen," he said, and turned around. "You're just going to sit in the car and hold the steering wheel and that's it. You don't have to crawl under it and work on it."

He couldn't find the old chain he thought he still had from years ago so he took the bag of tire chains he had never used and tossed it into the back of the camper.

"Let's go."

The road was old. It was narrow. The land on either side was flat. Small communities of blacks lived along the road, left over from the days of tenant farming. Each community had a church. After church, the black families walked back down the road to their houses. They were dressed in their best clothes. As they walked, they paraded their finery, and waved and talked back and forth to each other on either side of the road and to the families already gathered in the front yards of their houses. They barely minded the cars coming down the road.

"Get the fuck off the road," Ervin said through the windshield.

"Don't talk like that around me," Margaret said.

"Look at them. We gave them the vote, we gave them the schools, and then we gave them all our jobs and they're still just niggers."

"I won't listen to that," she said. She turned her face to the side and smiled pleasantly at the people they passed, hoping to counter Ervin's scowling looks.

"The ones over in Korea weren't so bad," he said, remembering blacks he had fought with, "but I guess it was just the army keeping them in line."

"You used to write to, what's his name, you know, when you first got back."

"Yeah, but he was different."

"What ever happened to him?"

"How should I know? Things are different now. He's probably got uppity by now, like the rest of them."

"You were nicer then, to everybody," she said, thinking about herself in particular, and feeling awfully discouraged about what they had lost. "We had such a happy family."

"Don't get started on that crap," he said. "You're just here because I need someone to drive the car. I didn't bring you along to have to listen to that weepy crap about the way we used to be."

"You better be nice to me or I won't drive."

"If you won't drive, I'll leave you out there all alone and then you'll see how nice your black folks are."

"Do it," she said. "I want you to. I wouldn't have a minute's trouble. They can tell what I think of them. They can tell I'm not prejudiced."

"Bull," he said and slowed down. "After we get stopped just get in the car and I'll hook us up and pull us home. You steer and when you see me hold my hand up, like this, it means I'm getting ready to put on the brakes."

"Then what?"

"Then you get ready to put on yours so you won't ram into the back of me."

"The power brakes won't work with the motor off, will they?"

He let her out. He backed up to within a few feet of the old car. He took out the tire chains, hooked them together and managed about five feet of length and then hooked one end over the ball of the trailer hitch on the camper and the other around the bumper of the car.

"Put it in neutral, here," he said and reached in and did it, "and take off the emergency brake," he said and reached down and did that for her, too, but in doing so touched her leg. "Get out of the way. Move over. I can't get the brake off."

"Drive slowly," she said.

"I will."

The car was so close to the camper that Margaret could not see the road between them. She felt as if she were going to ram into the back of the camper and almost immediately, she waved her hand for him to stop.

He looked in his outside rearview mirror and saw her and rolled his window down and waved her away. He took it up to forty-five miles an hour and checked back. She was still waving her hand so he gave her the braking signal and pulled over on the shoulder.

"What is it?"

"I can't do it. I can't see the road. I can't see where you're going or which way the road is going up ahead. All I can see is the back of the camper."

"We can't stop now," he said. "Just follow me. That's all you have to do."

He got back in and took it up to fifty. Margaret quickly looked at the speedometer, afraid to take her eyes off the camper, and when she saw how fast he was going, applied the brakes. They had little effect though she mashed as hard as she could.

He felt the car drag and waved his arm back and forth and she let off. He took it up to sixty then and the car began to tremble, like the steering wheel was going to shake loose.

"I can't make it," she said out loud to herself. "He's got to stop." She rode the brakes steadily. Ervin felt it and took it up to seventy, grinning as his big V-8 overcame the drag behind him.

At seventy, the old car began to shake as if it were coming apart. Margaret forgot all about the brakes and just held on for dear life to the steering wheel, which shook so violently it jiggled the loose flesh under her arms and on her face like she was hooked up to the belt of an exercise machine. She held on tighter and she opened her mouth so she could breathe better. She looked like she'd grabbed a high-voltage wire as her cheeks slopped back and forth like an old woman with a bad case of palsy.

Ervin looked in his rearview mirror and thought, What the hell, and then remembered how badly out of balance the front tires were and he chuckled and took it up to seventy-five.

"Oh Jesus, help me get through this," she warbled in vibrato like a singer on a warped recording.

The camper and the car sped by the black families on the side of the road and in their front yards. The two vehicles drew attention not only by their speed but by their extreme proximity and by the smoke and smell of burning asbestos as Margaret mashed on the brakes.

In the front yard of an old frame house with a sagging front porch and a cleanly swept dirt front yard and a giant green John Deere tractor parked beside the house, and nearly larger than the old dwelling, which sat on the edge of a field owned by the farmer who owned the little house and the tractor, as well, the extended clan of the old couple who lived there stopped in midsentence as they heard the approaching vehicles and, like the teeth of a gear rotating slowly, all turned and watched the sight.

"What's that coming?" one of them asked.

"I don't know."

"There it come," the first one said.

"Look," another said.

"I never seed nothing like that before," the first one said, pointing as the two vehicles sped by with what looked like the driver of the first one laughing and the driver of the second crying.

"Is that man pulling that car?"

"Yeah. He pulling it."

"What's that smoke?"

"He burning up his engine."

"Must be them white folks from up North, going South for the winter," one of them suggested.

"Yeah," the first one said, satisfied with the explanation. "They always is in such a hurry."

When they got to the edge of town Ervin put out his hand and signaled, braked and slowed down. He kept to the speed limit once inside the city, and as the car stopped shaking, so did Margaret, so that by the time they got to the parking lot of Wart's garage, the only signs of her fright were the dried tracks her tears had made in her makeup.

"I will never talk to you again," she said when she got out on shaky legs.

"Of course you will."

"I will never do anything for you again. Don't even ask."

"Don't blame me if you don't know how to drive. You are the one who got scared and quit driving."

"I want to go home. Take me home."

"And look what you did to the bumper, putting on your brakes when you weren't supposed to." He pointed to the bumper, which had bent out like the prow of a ship.

"Just take me home."

Back in the house, Ervin turned on the NFL, got a Coke from the refrigerator and a bag of Doritos, nacho flavor, and settled down for a perfect afternoon.

Margaret went into her room, took off her coat, took off her shoes and sat on the edge of the bed. She remained there in the stillness of the darkened room, trying to ignore the football game in the other room, and trying to decide what next to do.

Five

Friday, coming home from work early, Sally and Robert began scraping. The house was a story and a half. It was in two sections. The sections were built into each other and formed a T. The back section had a large dormer on both sides of the roof. The roof was tin and painted red. The rest of the house was basically one story.

She had decided to paint it a pure yellow-ochre color, a deep and rich yellow that was like the most golden color of the sun before it turned red.

They scraped until their arms ached, getting nowhere with the stubborn, old lead-based paint. They went inside to rest and saw, while glancing through a Sears catalog, a paint sprayer with a sandblasting attachment.

"Let's get it tomorrow morning," she said.

The old truck, a 1955 Dodge, wouldn't make it the forty-five miles to Durham so they took her car. When they got to the store they discovered the one advertised on sale wouldn't handle a sandblaster well enough for what they needed, so they bought a five-hundred-dollar outfit with the intention of selling it when they finished with it.

After they got all the way back home Robert couldn't make the plug fit.

"It's for a two-twenty outlet," the salesman said when they called him.

They loaded the heavy thing back into the trunk and drove back to Durham.

"You'll have to buy this five-horsepower gasoline-powered model," the salesman told them.

"It'll sandblast?" Sally asked.

"Absolutely."

A man in bib overalls was listening to the conversation. He had a paper cup in one hand. About the time the salesman went off to do the paperwork, the man spit into the cup and came over to Robert and Sally.

"Was you talking about sandblasting?" he asked.

"Yeah," Robert answered.

"You going to use that?"

"Yeah."

"Of course it's none of my business, but I don't believe I'd do that if I was you."

"Why not?" Sally asked.

The man had on a cap with a frayed bill exposing the cardboard within and the cap had an emblem on the front with two rebel flags crossed like swords and the faded words, "Martinsville Speedway," above the flags.

"It won't last," he said and looked down at Sally and more or less into the bill of his cap, as if talking to a strange woman was a difficult thing. "It just won't hold up no time at all. Them seals go bad, see. That engine's aluminum. It can't take much heat."

"Well, what would you suggest?"

"Buy mine. I got one I'll sell you for the same as that."

He spit into the cup and even though Sally tried not to, she saw the filthy brown tobacco juice.

"I don't really want to sell it," he said, "but I got down in my back a few months ago and can't use it no more."

"Where can we see it?" Robert asked.

"Over at my place."

"Where's that?"

They talked it over and then Robert said, "Well, we weren't really planning to spend quite that much when we came over here."

"I can sell it to you for less."

"It'd have to be a lot less."

"We can talk about it," the man said.

After the salesman refunded their money, they followed the man out to an old Ford pickup with homemade wooden sides piled to the top with pieces of machinery and old tires.

"My name's Delbert Johnson, by the way," he said, leaning out the window. They followed him for miles. They drove completely out of Durham and then out of Durham County and onto Highway 70 and west for ten more miles, then north beyond Hillsborough.

"Bad sign," Robert said.

"You want to stop?" she asked.

"Too late now."

"I guess we might as well see what he's got."

Finally Delbert stopped and pointed to a narrow, rutted driveway that was worse than theirs. A couple of hundred feet down they suddenly came to a clearing. The house was one story with asphalt siding. The siding had been manufactured with a brick-veneer pattern. In the yard were two pulp-wood trucks, a dozen old cars and a pile of machinery and appliances and lumber that just went on as far as they could see.

"Bad news," Sally said.

Six dogs came out from under the house. They ran at the car. Delbert yelled and threw a radiator hose at them. "Don't mind them, folks. Just go ahead and get out. They won't bother you none."

"You've got a lot of stuff here," Robert said.

"I save everything and anything. You wouldn't believe what people throw away."

They walked behind the house. The dogs sniffed them.

One of them rammed his nose up Robert's ass and then walked around in front of him and looked him in the eye as if he'd smelled something peculiar and wanted to check out the face that went with the smell.

"Here it is," said Delbert. He pointed to a four-cylinder diesel air compressor mounted on a two-wheel trailer. "It's old but it'll really do a job."

"But what is it?" Sally asked. "I mean, what was it?"

"It's an old state-surplus compressor. They used them to run jackhammers to tear up roads."

"It's bigger than we imagined," she said.

"Yes ma'am, but you need it if you're going to sand-blast."

The machine was buried in vines and blackberry briars. They couldn't see it clearly.

"Let me get my old Farmall and pull her loose," he said and set off at a limping trot toward a shed, like Grandpappy Amos on "The Real McCoys."

"We're in trouble," Robert said.

"Let's just look at it and be polite and then hurry on back to Sears and get the other."

Sally looked back at the house. She saw a woman standing in an open doorway. The woman stared at her. She waved. The woman never moved. Delbert came back. He was driving a rusty old Farmall-A tractor, and dragged a chain behind it which he hooked to the trailer to pull it free of the growth.

"We'll have to jump her off." He attached the jumper cables to the tractor battery. "They're both six-volt," he said and got a can off the porch and came back, looking over his shoulder at the woman.

"Don't worry about her. That's my wife's mother."

He returned to the porch and filled a can with oil from the tank on stilts beside the house.

"Heating oil is the same as diesel fuel," he said and then sprayed ether from an aerosol can into the air cleaner and mashed the starter.

Blue smoke puffed and wheezed out of the stack on top of the engine but it wouldn't start.

"It'll start, I swear it will. I had that thing running just the other day."

Delbert's mother-in-law appeared in front of them.

"Will you be wanting lunch?"

"Not yet."

"It's lunchtime."

"Just not yet, that's all," he said and straightened up from the motor.

The old woman walked off.

"She don't talk much," Delbert said and went back to work.

He tried the starter again. The motor fired.

"I told you," he said.

The noise was so loud they couldn't think. Delbert pointed to a set of gauges and explained how they worked. He dragged a long red rubber hose from under the machine. He hooked it onto the air outlet, all the while talking incomprehensibly. He put a tire chuck on the end of the hose and filled the slack tires of the trailer on which the whole thing sat. It was an enormous steel trailer with a tongue that had been resting on a concrete block before he pulled it out of the bushes.

After he filled the tires, he went into the bushes and came back with a splattered paint sprayer and hooked it up. It worked. Then, with the motor still wide-open and the heavy diesel smoke settling around the house and yard like fog, he hooked up the sandblasting attachment. He sprayed from an old bucket. He sprayed the bushes. Branches ripped off like they'd been machine-gunned, leaving the bushes bare and stripped. Then he cut off the motor and looked over at them and laughed.

"I told you, boy. I told you it'd work. I just bet you didn't believe me when you saw it. Now tell me. Did you?"

"We weren't sure," said Robert, the first words either of them had spoken in the half-hour, mind-rattling display.

"It'll eat up that little Sears machine and spit out the parts," he said and laughed again.

"Can we talk about it?" Robert asked Delbert.

"You just suit yourself," he said.

"It worked," Sally said.

"I know, but . . ." he said.

"But it worked. It really did."

"You mean you want to buy it?"

"Why not? We can strip the paint off the house this afternoon and have it painted twice before Thursday."

"And then what?"

"Sell it."

"Let's do it, then."

"How much do you want for it?" she asked.

"I'll take six hundred. Everything included."

After he said that, he let fall a wet, black, compacted mass of chewed-up tobacco. It rolled out of his mouth and fell like a dog turd onto the ground. He spit. He stuck his finger in his mouth and wiped out the insides of his cheeks. He pulled a single toothpick from his shirt pocket and used it and then took a pouch of tobacco from the other shirt pocket and mashed in a fresh chaw.

"That's too much," Robert said.

"We can't afford that."

"How much can you afford?" Delbert mumbled through the tobacco.

"About two hundred," Robert said.

"Done," he said and grabbed Robert's hand and shook it. "A handshake's good enough for me," he said.

After he shook his hand he leaned to one side and spit a stream of fresh juice that looked like some kind of liquid disease.

"Can I write you a check?" Sally asked.

"I can't cash no check," he said, more to Robert than her. "I don't have no bank account."

Robert had that much in his wallet, having just cashed his paycheck.

"I've got it," he mouthed to Sally, who nodded for him to pay him, after which it occurred to him that they had no way to pull it back to their house.

"Can you pull it for us with your truck?" he asked.

"No sir, I can't do that. I'd like to, but what with the wife sick and all, I just can't."

"Well, how are we going to get it home? If you can't get it home," Sally said, "you'll have to give us our money back."

"Now it's not my fault about that," Delbert said, suddenly getting tough. "But I tell you what I'll do. I'll drag it over to the front and help you hook it up to your car. It won't be no trouble."

He pulled it with the tractor. The tongue dragged the ground and plowed a furrow as it went. It took all three of them to lift the heavy tongue and get it level with the bumper of the car.

"I thought you had a trailer hitch," Delbert said.

"Nope."

"Well, never mind. I'll work something out."

Robert held the tongue steady on top of the bumper while Sally pushed from behind to keep it from rolling away. Delbert returned with some electric-fence wire. He tied the tongue to the bumper and then wrapped it around and around and through the bumper and through every hole and slot he could find. When they stepped back, they saw that the weight of the tongue had flattened the back springs of the car and raised up the front so that it looked like a speedboat at full throttle.

"She's heavy, all right," Delbert said.

"You think we'll make it?" Sally asked.

"Sure. Just take it easy."

They started off. After a few feet, Robert applied the

brakes. The trailer slid forward and rammed into the back of the trunk.

"Hold a second," Delbert said and ran toward the house. He looked on the ground and then ran to the porch and saw one of his grandchildren's toys, a brown, furry teddy bear. He mashed it in between the trailer tongue and the trunk. The bear squeaked when he mashed it in.

"That'll keep from scratching that up," he said and off they went. All the way down the drive they heard the little bear squeaking as the trailer rammed back and forth against the trunk. At the state road they went around and looked.

"Jesus H. Christ," Robert said. "What have we done?"

"I don't know."

They leaned against the car. Through the trees they heard Delbert's tractor.

"I feel stupid," Sally said.

"Yeah."

"I guess it's not going to fall off, though," she said, pulling on it.

"You want to go?"

"Might as well. At least it'll work. Do we have enough sand?"

"He said we did."

"Let's go, then."

They crept along until they found Highway 70 and had been on it no more than a minute when they had a line of cars behind them. They were going thirty miles an hour. The temperature gauge in the car read danger.

"I've got to stop," he said.

"Wait until we find a good place," she said, looking back at the machine as it lumbered from side to side no matter how they tried to keep it straight. The bear squeaked and squealed and screamed, "Help, help," as the car lurched and jerked over the bumpy road. The weight of the trailer made the front end so light they had hardly any steering.

Soon the bear quit crying. Soon after that they pulled over at a roadside picnic table.

"Oh hell," he said.

"Look at that," she said, as the line of cars accelerated past them.

The trailer had crashed through and wedged into the trunk. The tongue had mashed the little brown bear through the metal. The end of the hitch stuck through its stomach.

They drove the rest of the way as if they were returning from the funeral of a close friend. The trailer, wedged firmly now, pulled better and they made it home without additional trouble.

After they got it loose from the car and jacked the tongue level they got out their jumper cables. The dog dreamily sniffed the wheels of the trailer, mesmerized by years of strange urine.

They hooked the jumper cables up and tried to start it. The cables melted. Robert went to buy new ones while Sally climbed the ladder and began scraping.

"I'll just kill some time doing this," she said.

When he returned with the heavier cables it still wouldn't start. He remembered the ether.

"I better go get some," he said.

"I'll just keep scraping," she said.

"Back to town," he said.

"Yep," she said.

With the ether the engine fired and then died. It kept firing and then dying.

"Damnit," Sally said.

"I know what it is," he said.

"What?"

"No fuel. It must have leaked out."

"I'll do a little more scraping," she said.

"Be right back."

He put the fuel in and then sprayed some more ether. It

turned over but would not start. He called a mechanic who had a shop nearby.

"You've got air in the lines," he told him.

"Is that bad?"

"It's not bad," the mechanic said. "It's just that a diesel won't start with air in the lines."

"What do I do?"

"You'll have to bleed them."

"Could you tell me how?"

"I can't explain it over the phone. You got to bring it on over here if you want me to do it now. I can't leave the shop and I hate to work Saturdays anyway."

Robert told Sally about the conversation.

"This is madness," she said.

"I'm sure not going to try to pull that thing anywhere again," he said.

"No. We can't do that."

"Well. What then?"

"Let's just quit. Let's just forget the house and forget the compressor."

"But we can't. The house looks worse than ever now, half scraped like that."

"I don't care. I mean, so what? Really. What difference does it make?"

"But."

"But I know. It was my idea."

"What'll we do with this old piece of junk, then? We can't leave it here."

"Get the truck and drag it around behind the barn. Maybe we can sell it. Maybe it'll start when it gets covered with vines."

For a moment before he moved it, their house took on the look of a Delbert Johnson homestead, in its early stages.

Later, after resting, they began scraping again, and did it all day Sunday as well and started painting Sunday night. Her parents were coming Thursday.

Six

Ervin's car was fixed right away. His points had broken in half. Wart fixed that and mashed the bumper in and the car was back in service. On Tuesday, as Ervin walked down the hall to leave the post office, he glanced out the window and saw Angie waiting for the bus.

Minutes later, Angie turned as she heard tires screeching and saw Ervin's car coming around the corner. It pulled into the road a half block ahead of the bus and stopped in front of her.

"Need a ride?" he asked.

"Sure," she said and got in. "Which way are you going?"

"Any way you want."

"Well, I'm going home. To the Brookstone Apartments."

"I know where they are," he said, and started off.

The bus pulled up behind him, and the crowd that had been waiting boarded. Ervin watched them in the rearview mirror.

"I didn't know you rode the bus," he said.

"I don't usually. My car's completely broken down. The guy says it'll cost too much to fix. More than it's worth."

"What'll you do?" he asked.

"Save my money and get another one. Later."

He got into the left lane and the bus pulled up beside him. It was packed and toward the back people were standing.

"I don't mean any disrespect by this," he said, nodding at the bus, "but you're new in this area and all that, and you wouldn't know, but down here, people just don't ride the bus."

"What do you mean?" she asked, looking at a bus full of people.

"I mean white people don't ride the bus. It's just not safe. That's why I rushed around to get you."

"Oh," she said, with a puzzled look on her face.

"Where are you from, anyway?"

"Originally from Cleveland," she said, "but I lived in Fayetteville for five years. My ex-husband was stationed at Fort Bragg. Still is, I should say."

"I see," he said.

"I took the postal exam shortly after we separated and then when I got a notice about this job, my daughter and I moved here."

"Uh huh," he said, now having to imagine the daughter as well as the ex-husband.

"She's seven," she said. "And a real sweetheart."

"I bet," he said.

"Here it is," she said, and pointed to Building C. "And there's my little girl. Waiting with Mrs. Scholtz at the bus stop."

"Who's Mrs. Scholtz?"

"She's a retired woman who keeps Darlene after school."

"I see."

"And there," she said and pointed to a rusty old Plymouth sedan, "is my old heap. Dead on its feet."

"That reminds me," he said. "I know a pretty good mechanic I could take the car to, if you want a second opinion."

"It's not worth it. It was Bill's car. I knew it wasn't any good when he gave it to me, but it was all I could hope for from the settlement."

"Well then, how about this? I'll take you home every afternoon."

"Can you do that?"

"Sure."

"I'll pay for the gas, then."

"No way."

"You've got to let me do something," she said.

"It'll be my pleasure. I like to help people. If I can do something nice for someone, it just makes my day."

"All right, then," she said. "See you tomorrow."

After he drove off, he thought, How stupid am I, I didn't arrange for her to get to work in the morning. She still has to take the bus then.

He was so excited about this new arrangement that instead of going home he drove to a 7-Eleven across town, where he bought a Coke, two oatmeal cookies and a Hershey's Big Block and celebrated. Then he went home, saw Margaret in the backyard working in the garden and turned away when she waved. He took out the Tupperware pitcher with the tea in it, already sweetened and lemoned, and poured a glass. As he sipped, he watched her working in the plant bed and noticed the flex and pull of her thighs as she bent over.

He put the tea pitcher back and turned the cap around past the notation for closed, past the notation for pour, and positioned it so that the top would fall off when the next person used it.

"How do you get to work in the morning?" he asked Angie that afternoon.

"I caught a ride this morning with Mrs. Scholtz's daughter. She said she could take me mornings if I was out there at the same time."

"Good," he said.

"She didn't seem to mind taking a dollar from me," she said, and held one out for him.

"No ma'am. Not for anything would I take it. This is on me."

Angie was twenty-seven and had married her husband, after she was pregnant, when she was nineteen. She had never known, in any way, really, another man. Her husband had been rough, hard-drinking and demanding, and Ervin's politeness, his courtliness, she thought, like an old Southern gentleman, delighted her.

"You're very kind. I don't pretend that money isn't precious to me."

"Of course it is. A single girl, all on her own. Of course it is," he said. "Now we won't say another word about it."

"All right."

He was late coming home again Wednesday, the second day in a row, and although Margaret had said nothing about it yesterday, she wasn't going to let it slide by today.

"You're late," she said when he came in.

"Late for what?"

"You know what I mean."

"How can I be late when there's nothing to be late for?"

"Listen," she said. "You were late yesterday. You had a funny look on your face. You're late today. For the past, I don't know how many years, you've come home like clockwork, so don't tell me you don't know what I mean."

He began whistling a song and walked over to the window. He whistled old songs, such as "Annie Laurie" or "Old Folks at Home," which Margaret used to love to hear as she lay with her head on his shoulder while they drove along, young and in love.

Now, though, he used the songs to block her out, to mock her, and when he struck up with "Row Row Row Your Boat," she screamed at him.

"Stop that damn whistling." She pulled him by the arm so that he had to look at her. "You better not be messing around."

"Oh?"

"You know what I told you."

"What did you tell me?" he asked and walked into the kitchen, where he opened the refrigerator door and looked in.

"You know."

"I can't remember," he said in a childish voice. "Please tell me again so I'll know."

"I'll not do it," she said.

"Sorry," he said, and walked to the back door.

"Where are you going?"

"To the mall. They're having a sale. I want to check out the fishing tackle."

"Take me with you."

"No," he said in a whining voice. "I don't want to take you with me."

"I want to go. I never go anywhere. I never get out of the house all day."

"That's not my fault. Get your license back."

"Just wait a minute while I get dressed."

"Sorry," he said. He let the storm door slam. The Plexiglas panels rattled as if they were going to fall out.

She ran at him, still in her housecoat and bare feet. He sprinted to the car. He jumped in. She pulled on the passenger door handle but it was locked.

"Ha ha, got you," he said through the closed window. She beat on the window.

"I can't hear you," he said and held his hand to his ear the way he had done with Angie that time. He started the engine. She ran around and stood with her knees against the back bumper.

"Get out of my way," he screamed with an ugly, red face.

"If I can't go, you can't go," she screamed back.

He rolled his window partway down and yelled, "I'm going to run over you. I'm going to kill you if you don't move."

"Go ahead. You want to, anyway. You've wanted to for years."

He put the car in neutral and stomped the accelerator to the floor. The car shook against her legs as if she were really stopping it.

"KILL ME," she screamed. "GO AHEAD AND DO IT," she yelled at him through the back window.

He let off on the gas momentarily, put the car in reverse and then, with his foot down hard on the brake, stomped the accelerator again. The car twisted and reared up on one side. Black smoke poured out the tail pipe. Particles of metal and rust from the exhaust sprayed all over her.

"GET OUT OF THE WAY," he yelled.

"DO IT," she screamed, and then, trembling like the car itself as it began to die out, she said again, more quietly, "Go on and do it."

The motor idled roughly and then died. Ervin got out. "Okay," he said. "You win. Get dressed. We'll go to the mall and have supper and do some shopping."

With her head held high, she went in the back door. Ervin leaned against the trunk of the old car, which he had bought from the city when it sold its worn-out police cars. On the ground behind the tail pipe was a bare spot where the force of the exhaust had cleared away all the pine straw. In the spot, which was as clean as if it'd been swept, he noticed the soot and bits of metal.

Damn near blew up my engine, he thought, and looked toward the house. Margaret was standing at the window, still in her housecoat.

"Go get dressed," he said and waved her away.

She left. He looked over his shoulder. The couple who lived next door were standing at the window. He waved to them. They waved back. They left the window. Hope you enjoyed the show, he thought, and looked around to see if anyone else was watching. He looked across his yard. The yard had no grass. It was covered with needles from the longleaf pines. The longleaf pines dropped pinecones, as well. Margaret gathered them and made displays, or dried them and varnished them, thinking to give them as presents. The closets and attic were full of them.

The neighborhood was quiet now, as if with the death of the roaring engine, all other sound had ceased as well. He heard water running, a distant gurgling sound that came, he decided as he looked at the house, from the vent pipe in the roof over her bathroom.

She's just flushed the toilet, he thought, and in a quick move, got in the car and backed out. She heard the engine. She ran for the door.

"You promised," she yelled as she opened it and saw him doing down the street.

"Come back," she said and chased him and nearly caught him by cutting catty-corner across the yard but he zoomed off and she found herself standing on the side of the road, abandoned and betrayed.

"I'll just walk," she said, and set off toward the mall. If he's not there, she thought, then I'll know he's running around on me, and if he is, she told herself, making a fist, there'll be trouble.

Ervin drove into the Fast Fare and bought a Coke and oatmeal cookie and a package of six miniature powdered doughnuts. He ate while he drove around and then, actually on the way to the mall, saw Margaret, walking barefoot, on the shoulder of the road. He parked and watched her. She never turned around. She walked with determination, as if she meant to get there.

I can make it, she told herself. I haven't walked this far since we went to New England twenty years ago but I can do it. She stepped on a sand spur, a ball of spikes. She balanced on one foot and pulled it loose from the other.

Damn fool, Ervin thought, and drove up beside her. She looked away.

"Get in."

"I'm going to the mall."

"Barefoot? In the dark? In the cold?"

"So what?" she asked, and held herself as dignified as one could, given the circumstances.

"Just get in the car," he said. "You don't even have your damn purse with you."

"I guess I showed you," she said. They started home.

"I guess I showed you," she said again.

"You didn't show me a thing I didn't already know," he said.

"Some men tried to pick me up," she said.

"Oh really?"

"Yes. Back at that house, with all the cars in the front yard. I was walking along and they called to me."

"What did they say?"

"They said something nasty."

"Uh huh."

"They did. They wanted me to come inside with them."

"Pretty damn hard-up men, I'd say. Yelling at a fat, fifty-four-year-old woman."

"I'm not fat."

"Hell."

"They liked me."

"Sure thing," he said. "Tell me another one," he said and laughed all the way home.

Seven

Sally and Robert painted Monday and Tuesday after work and then stayed home Wednesday and finished most of the second coat by that afternoon. Sally left him and went to town to the grocery store to buy what she needed for Thanksgiving.

The traffic moved slowly and she was mad, not at the traffic or the house or the painting or Robert or even the visit, but at herself and another damn period starting.

Of course, it was not the end of the world. It could be considered a new beginning. It could be looked at that way, the way losers were taught to look at things so they wouldn't drive right off the bridge or pull out the gun; it could be looked at that way if you were a believer with the kind of faith that allowed the fourteen-inch fist of a nonbeliever to be jammed through your teeth and halfway down your throat while you stood in front of him spouting the words of holy men.

It was the operation, of course, that was to have fixed all that, and damnit all, it did nothing, just ripped her up some more. Damn the faith healers and the holy medical men and their healing powers and damn the sales pitch heavy with the syrup of sucked blood, engorged with the tumescent bulge of wallets throbbing with the thrill of another surgical procedure and damn the spinal paralysis of the long needle, the foolish conversation of Valium-induced merriment and damn the promise of that zero-to-forty-percent chance looking better all the time in the narcotic dreams in front of her eyes, the promise of tubes so clean and swift eggs would dance and sing their way to conception, and all the infections of the past would be gone.

Damn all those things Sally Zilman thought as the traffic moved slowly, the line turning into the parking lot moving in coordination with the line at the other end leaving the lot, as if there were only room for one car entering as one left, only room in the store for one person as another left.

Soon she found a space. She bought a fresh turkey and stuffing mix and cranberries and sweet potatoes and a bag of marshmallows and a bottle of wine. She bought and she bought, knowing she had to because everyone expected all the right things.

Thursday morning they both painted furiously and by ten o'clock they were finished and the latex paint would dry in a few hours.

"Now," she said, "I've got my house the way I want it."

At eleven, her parents arrived.

"They must have left at daybreak," Robert said, "or before."

"Well, they're here. Let's go."

By the time they got to the camper, Ervin stood beside it with the door closed and Margaret nowhere in sight.

"Where's Mother?"

"She won't get out."

"Why not?"

"Because I won't open the door for her."

"Well, go open it," Sally said.

"I can't."

"I will, then," she said. "Come out, Mother."

"Not until your father opens it and helps me down."

"But Mother. He never does that. He never has."

"He used to. He will again."

"She won't get out," Sally said to Robert and her father.

"Let her sit," her father said and grabbed the handles of his new cooler, which was as big and heavy as a baby's coffin.

"Steaks," he said.

"Steaks? For Thanksgiving?" Robert asked.

"For tomorrow morning. Steak and eggs."

Ten minutes later, inside, the three of them stood in the kitchen talking when Sally, who could bear it no longer, asked her father if he noticed anything different about the house.

"Looks like you finally painted it," he said, and flipped open the cooler. "Bright color, that yellow."

She walked out so as not to blow up in front of him. She opened the camper door, where her mother rested her feet on the dash. It was warm inside.

"I'm a flower," she said. "I need a lot of attention."

"We're all flowers, Mother."

"And your father's a tree. He's hard and brittle, like the rough bark of a tree."

"Okay. That's fine," she said. "You're a flower and he's a tree but let's get out and get on with the day."

"I will not."

"Well, if you won't get out, then at least tell me what you think about the house."

"I think it looks a lot better but I wouldn't have painted it yellow," she said. "But it does look better."

"Thanks a lot," Sally said.

"Tell him to come get me. He'll listen to you."

"I will, but why all this now?"

"Because I saw this couple on the Donahue show and the woman said their marriage worked because her husband still treated her like he was courting her and I thought, Of course,

I'll treat him that way if he'll treat me that way, but he has to start first. He stopped first, so he has to start back first.''

Forty-five minutes later Sally persuaded her father to get her.

"Come on," he said.

"Take my hand," she said and extended it. "Help me down properly."

He took it. He had to fight off the impulse to jerk her to the ground and stomp on her.

"Thank you," she said. She walked in like a grand lady on escort.

"Don't thank me," he said and leaned close and whispered, "because when we get home I'm going to fix you but good."

"Of course, you'll do no such thing," she said.

"Now that wasn't so bad, was it, Daddy?"

"It was bad enough."

"He's stubborn," Margaret said.

"Do you help your wife in and out of the car?" he asked Robert.

"I would, I guess, if she wanted me to."

"Hear, hear," Margaret said and Ervin left the house. He wandered around in the yard and looked at the house and thought what a godawful hippie color they had painted it. He stood with his back to it and wanted to smoke, but put it out of his mind and just walked around waiting for the women-folk to get the glands calmed down. Hell to pay, he thought, on those certain days, and felt sorry for all the men in the world like himself who tried to do battle with female hormones.

Around the back of the barn he came upon the Delbert Johnson landscape.

"What's that?" he asked back inside.

"That," Sally said, "is exactly what it looks like."

"A piece of junk?"

"It is an air compressor that we used to scrape and paint

the house," she said, which was, in the distant reaches of
the truth, accurate, because they had used it to force them to
scrape and paint it.

"You never," her father said. "That old thing wouldn't
blow my hair."

Boy, just give me the chance, Robert thought. I'd blow
you into a damn hole and cover you up.

"Suit yourself," Sally said and went on with cooking.
They ate at three-fifteen. The wine loosened them up. Her
father soon started the jokes. At first, they were not too bad.

"How many Carolina students does it take to change a
light bulb? Three. One to hold the bulb, one to unscrew it,
and one to hold the beer."

After that, they got worse. Sally called time-out for dessert. Then it was time to clean up. Everyone helped. She
wanted to do it alone. She wanted them out of her kitchen.
Four people were too much. They were tight as if they were
crammed in a closet. They bumped and scraped by each
other and filled every horizontal surface with dishes and pots
and leftovers and glasses and plates of half-eaten pumpkin
pie.

They crawled over each other. Ervin began talking nonstop. He started in on the jokes again. Margaret switched to
her soap opera queen act and fixed a smile on her face, determined to be gracious.

From the other room, a football game on the television
laid a background of cheers and music, excited talk and so
forth. Georgia versus Alabama. Carolina versus Duke. Who
knew who was playing? Who cared?

Ervin reached over Sally. He grabbed at a dishtowel from
the rack over the sink. He mashed her into the cabinet. Margaret walked behind him and knocked him loose, pushing
him against Robert, who was already jammed into the corner
against the hot water heater, trying to stay out of the way.
They bumped each other around the room like people inside
a pinball machine.

"It's getting crowded in here," Ervin said, and began another joke. "Did you hear the one about the grapefruit?"

No one answered.

"See, there were these two boys walking down the street and one of them has this grapefruit in his hand and he takes out his pocket knife and he's getting ready to cut it open and eat it. Suddenly the other boy stops him and points up to a Jewish synagogue."

Oh shit, Robert thought. Here it comes.

"He says to the boy with the grapefruit, 'Don't you ever eat a grapefruit in front of a synagogue.' 'Why not?' the other one asks. 'Because if you do, all the juice will run out.' "

Ervin laughed. He was the only one laughing.

"Now that," his wife said, "was certainly not funny."

"You people wouldn't know funny if it hit you in the face," he said, turning on her fast.

Sally dried her hands. Robert looked down and thought, What do I do? Kill the old man, or what?

"Listen, Daddy," Sally said. "You're just going to have to stop it with those jokes. In this house, anyway, you're going to have to stop it."

"What for? They're just jokes. If a person can't joke about things, he might as well give up."

"Those aren't jokes, though," she said.

"No, they're not," his wife said and he glared at her.

"What are they, then?"

"Mean and vicious stories."

"You people are just knee-jerk liberals," he said. "Anything a nigger does is right and anything a white does is wrong."

"What's that got to do with it?" Robert asked.

"We're just talking about good manners, Daddy. We're talking about good manners and treating people with respect."

"Boy," he said. "The day my own daughter, who I taught how to have good manners from the day she was born . . ."

"What about me?" Margaret asked. "I taught her, too."

". . . from the day she was born, starts teaching me what's right and what's wrong, well, I tell you, that'll be the day."

He looked around the room. Robert looked at the floor. The two women looked at Ervin. "I can see I'm not wanted," he said. "I better leave if that's the case."

He walked to the door. On the way through, he said, without turning around, "I know exactly where I'll go," and he let the screen door shut by itself, pulled back quickly by the spring hooked to the jamb.

The dog and the cat had been waiting outside for the leftovers and as soon as he cleared the door, they charged in. The cat ran through the dog's legs and slowed him down and the door slammed on his hindquarters. He yelped, and slipped through.

"Is he really going?" Sally asked her mother.

"He better not be," she said as he drove off.

"That's a first," Robert said. "He's been out of control, but never that much."

"I think he's got a girlfriend," Margaret said.

"Not seriously, Mother. Not really."

"I think so. He's been coming home late."

"From work?"

"Yes. And he used to always come home at the same time. Like clockwork."

"Does he go out at night?"

"No."

"On the weekends?"

"No."

"Then when does he have time to have a girlfriend?"

"I think she must work with him."

"What makes you sure?"

"I've been married to him for thirty years."

"Oh."

"That's a pretty good argument," Robert said.

"Well, Mother, really, I'm sure it's nothing. Whatever he's doing, he's probably doing just to get at you."

"That doesn't make it hurt any less," she said.

"Just ignore him. I'll bet he'll stop."

"I can't ignore him."

Her lips quivered and her nostrils flared and turned red and she left the room.

"That's the saddest thing I've ever seen," Robert whispered. "He treats her like dirt and she still loves him."

"Of course she loves him, you stupid dope."

"Hey. Don't start on me. I'm not your father. I just can't see how she can still love him."

"She loves what they used to have. What we used to have. Together. As a family."

"But I mean, enough is enough."

"She wants it back. She can't let go of the idea that she can get it back. You remember my grandparents?"

"I never met them."

"I know, they've been dead for years, but what I'm trying to tell you," she said and looked toward the bathroom to make sure her mother was out of earshot, "was that she grew up in real bad circumstances."

"I knew that, I think."

"Her father was hard on her and her brothers. Real hard. And when she met Daddy and left to marry him, her whole world changed like she had only dreamed it would."

"She told you this?"

"Many times. She would take out the pictures of Daddy in his uniform before he was shipped off to Korea and talk about things back then. It was so good, coming from what was so bad, that to her, it's worth waiting for again."

"You guess."

"I guess."

"We don't really know."

"But I think I'm right."

"She could be planning to leave him any day now. She could have a lover."

"No way," Sally said. "That's not mother. That's just not her style."

Ervin drove to Chapel Hill. Along the way, yards full of cars and parents and children reminded him it was, indeed, Thanksgiving, the day to be with the family and give thanks for what one has.

Of course I'm thankful, he said to himself. I'm grateful for all I have. I'm no ingrate. That's one thing I'm not, he told himself and thought about Angie, probably alone, and how sweet it would be to be with her.

Everything was closed in town. There was nowhere to go. He eventually found a FastFare. He parked. He called Angie on the pay phone. There was no answer.

He went inside. He had eaten too much and the turkey was squawking around in his stomach like it was trying to get out.

"I sure would like a cigarette about now," he announced to the woman behind the counter as he entered. She wore a red-and-cream-colored FastFare smock and she was eating a candy bar and reading a magazine and sitting beside the cash register.

"What kind?"

"Oh I can't really do it. I just said I wished I could."

She looked back.

"I gave it up a few years ago. Just like that," he said and snapped his fingers. She nodded.

They were alone in the store. He stood in the middle of the checkout area. A large wood-look plastic tub full of ice and beer cans leaked on the floor just behind him. He moved his heel out of the water and heard a strange, electronic musical sound. He saw a single video game against the wall. It was called Pole Position. He walked over and, as if by magic, the moment he stopped in front of it, a voice came out of the machine and said, "Insert your quarter now."

It was an awkward, pinched voice, without pitch or variance. After it spoke, the music began again, and a trial run of the race started.

He put a quarter in the slot. A musical fanfare blasted the quiet store. The instructions rolled on the screen. He put the gearshift in low and applied his foot lightly to the pedal. The game began. He wiggled and twisted his hips as he maneuvered the car through the difficult and tricky course. Soon he shifted to high and soon after that wrecked his car for the last time. The game stopped. A voice said, "Game over. Insert your quarter now."

"Ah well," he said and turned to the woman. "I'm not as fast as I used to be, I guess."

He put his hands in his pockets and jingled his keys and walked to the aisle where the individual packs of cookies and cakes were. It was the same in every store. It was easy to find. As he walked over, he whistled, "Oh My Darling Clementine," and he wagged his head from side to side, keeping time.

Oh my darling, oh my darling, oh my darling Clementine, he thought as he whistled, you are lost and gone forever, he thought and then stopped whistling in front of the candy, still jingling the keys in his pocket.

"I really shouldn't have anything," he said out loud, and reached for a peanut butter Twix, which he had just seen on television and wanted to try. Just then a man rushed in the store and asked, looking all around, where the charcoal lighter was. The woman pointed and Ervin spoke up.

"It's over here," he said. "I'll show you."

The man thanked him, paid and left. Ervin walked over to the checkout counter.

"Is that all?" she asked.

"Yes. I believe it will be."

"Forty-one cents."

He paid her and then turned sideways to the cash register and peeled the wrapper off the two thin, chocolate-covered wafers and took a bite.

"You know, I've got a daughter about your age."

"Is that so?"

"Have you tried this new Twix yet?"

"Sure haven't," she said, without looking up.

After he finished the last bar he had a twinge of heartburn and went to the medicine aisle and bought a bottle of Maalox, which he took to the camper and drank straight from the bottle, as if it were soda pop.

It was six-thirty and dark when he returned. They heard him drive up. He looked at the house as he parked. He saw three faces in three separate windows.

"Well, I'm back," he said.

It was an awkward moment. It was as awkward for Robert as the time he threw up all over the girl beside him in third grade and then, after leaving the room to clean up, had to come back and sit beside her. He felt that embarrassed for the old man, who had essentially thrown up all over everyone, rushed out to clean up, and then returned.

It was awkward for Margaret, as she saw the remains of the man she married trying to crawl through the brambles they had grown around each other. She was sorry for him.

It was awkward for Sally, who wished she were not there and hadn't seen or heard all that she'd seen and heard that afternoon and wished that she were not going to be put in the middle and have to hear any more of it. She feared what would come next, and wondered how she would ever get away from this crazy family.

"Well," he said and cleared his throat, "what I've brought for you is this. I realized out there how good it was to have a family to come back to, and I've brought each and every one of you an apology. I apologize to you all if I hurt your feelings or said something wrong."

He crammed the apology down Robert's throat by walking

over and shaking his hand. He forced it into Sally by kissing her on the cheek and he floated over to his wife and put his arm around her and pulled her to him.

"Just one of those days," he said.

"Well," Sally said, becoming the arbiter of the family, "I guess that's what families are for."

"How's that?" Robert asked.

"They're places where you can look bad and make a fool of yourself and still come back to."

"Hey, here now," her father said. "Let's not go too far, how about it."

He laughed. He laughed hard enough to force a weak and polite laugh out of everyone else, and with the laughter things returned to normal, as normal as four naked people in a room could be.

Eight

The Neals left Friday just before lunch. Sally went to the garden and looked at the dead vegetable plants, withered tomato vines and the thick weeds.

"I think I'll turn the garden," she said when Robert came out to join her.

"I was going to."

"I'd like to. I need to shake the visit out of my system."

She went to the shed beside the old corncrib and, with one hell of a jerk that lifted the Rototiller off the ground, pulled the starter rope and fired the engine on the first try.

"At least this thing starts," she called over the noise and then walked the tiller on its tines across the side yard and across the driveway and into the garden. The soil was dry and hard. The tiller bounced on top of it and bounced her with it. Robert watched from the porch. The dog and the cat watched from the porch, too. After a few minutes, the tiller cracked through the red clay crust into the moist soil below.

She went down one row and up another. She stopped and untangled the weeds from the tines and began again. She rolled up her sleeves, tied her shirt at her waist and pulled her hair back and worked for an hour without stopping and had a third of the garden finished when the tiller ran out of gas. She got the can, filled it, and started again.

Robert walked into her line of sight. She stopped. She killed the motor.

"Take a break," he said.

"I'm going to finish. It makes me feel better," she said, and fired it up again with a single pull of the rope.

"I'll cook supper," he said. "When I see you're about finished, I'll run a hot bath."

She nodded and continued down the row. She finished. She took her bath. She ate. She felt relaxed, physically.

"But I'm pissed off," she said. "I don't think I'm going to be good company tonight."

"I guess it's not a good time to talk about how we're going to get out of going down there for Christmas, is it?"

"Not a good time," she said and went to bed, looking especially good to Robert, flushed and loose and fiery, just right, but no way, not tonight.

He turned on the television. "The Dukes of Hazzard" were on one station. "Washington Week in Review" was on another. He flipped back and settled down to watch Daisy Duke walk around in her short-shorts and try to keep her breasts inside her blouse. He wondered if this would be the night she and Bo and Luke finally made it on camera, cousins or no cousins.

Bo jumped the General Lee right over Hazzard County pond. Roscoe landed in the middle, sputtering and spitting water as he climbed on top of the car.

"He's all right," Luke said to Bo, looking back.

"Yeah. He's okay," said Daisy, who was in the back seat.

"Now let's do some fucking," said Bo, and Daisy took off her blouse and made room for Luke as he climbed back with her.

Ah, thought Robert. I was right. This is the night.

After Luke was through with her, Bo climbed in the back, and, as the scene faded, Daisy's legs appeared spread from one side of the car to the other and hooked over the back of the front seat. Bo disappeared from view. Robert climbed in through the window with Luke.

"Leave a little for me," Robert said to Bo. "I think I'm heading for a dry spell back home."

Daisy looked up from watching Bo work and said, "Sugar, come on back here right now. I've still got a mouth and two hands free."

"I think I'm going to have to move to Hazzard County," he said when it was all over and he looked in the bedroom where the light beside the bed cast a glow over Sally as she lay on her side with her long hair spread out like the halo of a glamorous movie star.

"But you know what happens around Christmas," she said to Robert Monday morning as they prepared to go to work. "Mother gets wackier and Daddy gets meaner."

"Well you tell me how we're going to get out of going and I'll back you up. They're your parents."

"Right."

"At least with mine, they know not to expect anything out of me. One visit a year."

"That's what comes from marrying me."

"Best thing I ever did."

"But Christmas, see, is this really tender time for Mother and she's already asked me to go to Christmas Eve services with her."

The matter remained unresolved when Robert left for work. He had to be there an hour before she did. He was doing trim work on a large apartment complex, and the job was big enough to last all winter, a good thing because it was all indoor work.

When Sally got to work she flipped on the lights. The fluorescent fixtures buzzed and flickered and then caught. She sat at her desk unenthusiastically as her eyes got used to the fizzy carbonated glow, and at exactly eight-thirty the

phone rang. It was Adrian. Adrian was a very particular cus-
tomer and she had fouled up a job for him.

"But it wasn't me," she told him.

"You're in charge."

"I suppose."

"Then it's just the same."

"What can I do about it now?" she asked.

"Do the whole job over."

"Impossible."

"Why?"

"Do you know, can you imagine how busy things get just
before Christmas, with the semester ending?"

"Yes, I can imagine, but my butt is on the line over here
and you put it there."

Disgusting, she thought. I wouldn't get near your butt for
anything.

"I can't do the job over. I just can't. Mistakes happen.
The announcement's not ruined, it's just not perfect."

"We shall see what you shall do and what you shall not
do," he said and hung up before she worked up the courage
to call him a tightass little pimp.

On the way home, looking for something to take her mind
off her work, she decided to begin writing in her journal
again, something she had let slide since the summer. It was
her secret project to document her life, for her own edifica-
tion only. Robert knew nothing about it, and it was best kept
that way. She tried to remember everything, and she tried to
make everything make sense. She made lists. She checked
one against the other. How many were on each side? Were
they equal. Did one good event weigh as much as one bad,
or as much as two? How to know?

She wrote about her parents. She wrote about men, and
men and women, and husbands and wives and fathers and
daughters and all the snaky trails left behind from the family
history, from stolen moments with strangers, a look, a kind

word, even, the gesture from someone never seen again that changed the day.

As Christmas grew closer, she withdrew more and soon Robert came down with the blues himself, just as if she'd given him the flu.

All of this went right over the head of Rocket, the cat, but Dreeno, the dog, knew something was up, and whenever either of them walked by, he looked sideways and weakly wagged his tail. He hated those long, drawn-out fights between the humans.

Nine

T.G. and Y. was a good store. It wasn't as big as K Mart, but it had good prices and different items, some that Ervin saw nowhere else. He went to the automotive section. On the shelves were cans of oil and gasoline additives. Some of the cans increased power. Some stopped annoying valve and push-rod noise. Some of them cleaned out carburetors. Some of them sealed cracked rings and overhauled worn-out engines as you drove.

He studied the labels. He held the cans at his waist and tilted his head back trying to bring the small print into focus. He bought a can of Marvel Mystery Oil and took it to his old police car. The engine needed something. Wart had told him his timing chain was worn out or the tensioner was worn out but he didn't want to put that kind of money in the car. He poured the additive into his crankcase and then started the engine. He could tell a difference. He went back to work. Later, he took Angie home.

"Can you stay awhile?" she asked.

"A few minutes, I guess."

He stayed longer than a few minutes and was home late again. Margaret was still in her bathrobe, same as when he'd left that morning.

"I just never got dressed. So what?"

"People don't stay in their pajamas all day unless they're sick, that's what. Are you sick?"

"No, and you're changing the subject. You used to come home almost exactly at five twenty-five every day, in time to see "The Andy Griffith Show," and now you come home almost any old time at all and don't even care if you miss it. That's what we're talking about."

She was hurt much worse than she was letting on. She had slipped into feeling tender toward him during the day and had made him a special Jello salad from a recipe she found in *Woman's Day*. She put in fruit chunks and nuts and cream cheese and then whipped it and chilled it and had already had a little bit, just to make sure it was as good as it looked, and she had it in the refrigerator waiting for him. But now, she thought, just for that, he's not going to have any.

Ervin got into the kitchen first. He opened the refrigerator and saw it.

"Look at that," he said. He took it.

"That's mine," she said. "You can't have any."

"Finders keepers," he said.

"Mine," she said and grabbed for it. He held it out of reach and went into his bedroom, eating it on the way.

"This is good."

"I made that for myself. You can't have any."

He shut the door in her face and she opened it just as fast.

"Get out of here. This is my room," he said and took another spoonful.

"I will not leave until you give me my Jello."

"You stay away from me or I'll throw it on the floor."

"I'm not leaving."

"Then watch me eat if you want to."

She walked toward him. He backed into his bathroom and locked the door.

"Open up."

He smacked his lips and sighed about how good it was.

"Open up and give it to me or I'll never cook you another thing. Never," she said, pulling on the door.

"Ah," he said, "this is something else. I better save the rest until I finish my shower," he said, as if talking to himself.

The water came on.

"You better let me in," she said. She pulled on the knob. She twisted it. She jerked on it. She put one foot on the wall and both hands on the doorknob and pulled as hard as she could and, to her great surprise, it came off in her hands and she fell backwards. The inside knob hit the tile floor.

"What are you doing?" he called and leaned out from behind the curtain. "What in the hell have you done now?" He picked up the broken knob. "You've torn it off. How in God's name did you do that?"

"I don't know," she said. "It just came off."

He looked through the hole in the door. The latch was still in. The door was still locked but there was no way to release the latch or unlock it.

"Put the knob back and see if you can turn it," she said.

"It won't go. Try yours."

"It won't either," she said. "It's locked from the inside, anyway."

"Then tell me, you stupid old bitch, just how the hell I'm going to get out of here."

"Maybe you're not."

"The hell you say."

"This is what you get for coming home late and taking my Jello."

"Cut the crap and get me out of here."

"Not yet," she said. "For once I've got you right where I want you."

"You don't have me anywhere."

"I think this is a good time to have a talk."

"Hell with the talk," he said and looked for something to turn the latch.

"You know," she said, sitting on the bed a few feet from the door, "the time just after we got married was the happiest of my life."

"I'm not listening," he said and stuck a toothbrush handle in the latch.

"They were happy times for you, too."

"I'm still not listening," he said. The plastic handle twisted without success.

There was no window. The bathroom had been a walk-in closet. It had been remodeled into his private bath when he started sleeping alone. The only ventilation was a fan built into the light. Like any closet door, it opened out and the hinge pins were on the outside.

"Do you remember how absolutely sweet we were with each other? Do you remember rushing home after work just to be with me? Do you remember that?"

"I can't hear you," he said. "The fan's making too much noise."

She sat on the floor and talked into the knob hole.

"Do you remember buying presents for me, for no reason at all, just because, you said, you adored me."

"ADORED SHIT," he screamed. "GODDAMN YOU, LET ME OUT OF HERE!"

"Not yet," she said calmly. "There's so much I want to talk about. Do you remember when I was pregnant with Sally? How happy we were. And when she was born?"

"I don't remember anything," he said, "and I can't hear you, anyway." He turned on the shower and the faucet at the sink.

"I know you can hear me even with the water running. I know you remember, too."

"Get me a screwdriver."

"Not until I'm finished."

"Listen you bitch. You go get me a screwdriver and unlock this door."

She sat on the carpet and leaned against the wall. She

pulled her robe over her knees and pulled her knees up to her chest. She held them against her with her arms crossed around them.

"The more you talk to me like that," she said in a calm voice, "the longer you'll have to stay in there."

"ARGHHHHHH," he screamed and went over to the toilet. When he heard her talking again he flushed it. Even with that, he could hear her and he put his fingers in his ears and hummed loudly, like a child drowning out a parent's lecture.

"I'm really serious, Ervin. It's time, it's really time for us to make up. It's just so wrong and so silly to waste what we had."

"Hummmmmm."

"You know, everyone makes mistakes. I've made some and you've made some, but people go on. They have to. You still love me. I know you do. And there's never been any other man for me but you."

"SHUT UP," he screamed.

"We don't even know what we're fighting about anymore. It's just a pattern, like a bad habit, and we've got to break it."

She looked through the hole and watched him and when he unplugged his ears and the toilet had filled, she spoke again.

"I read in a magazine about the need to break bad habits, how you just have to derail yourself off the bad track and get back on the good. You know what I mean?"

He looked at the ceiling and started whistling "Old Black Joe." She waited until he stopped and then asked, "Are you finished?"

"Are you?" he asked back.

This time, she did not answer.

"Okay. You're finished. You've had your say. Now get me the screwdriver."

Nothing.

"I know you're there." He turned off the water and the

fan. "I can hear you breathing. I know you're there so quit playing around."

He stuck his finger into the hole and picked on the latch. He hooked his fingernail into what he hoped would release the lock, and turned.

"Goddamnit, now look what you've made me do. I've broken my fingernail."

"You're like Br'er Rabbit. The harder you try, the more stuck you get."

"I knew you were there. Listen," he said, "this is dangerous. There could be a fire. I could be trapped in here."

"There won't be a fire."

The door was solid core. It would be difficult to break it down. If he broke it down, he thought, then he'd have to buy a new one.

"The Jello's melting," he said.

"I don't care about the Jello," she said, worn out and beginning to accept she would get nowhere. She pushed the screwdriver into the hole. He pulled it through, turned it around, inserted it in the slot he suspected would release the latch, and opened the door.

"Now get the hell out of my room," he said and twirled her around by her arm and pushed her into the hall. She went to the living room and put her palm on the cold windowpane. It was nearly Christmas. It didn't look it. The pine trees looked the same year round. It wouldn't snow. It rarely snowed in Wilmington. She wished she lived in the mountains, near the Blue Ridge Parkway, in a house that overlooked a valley. It would snow there, she thought, and as far as she could see would be white and clean and peaceful.

A car backed out of the driveway three houses down. The driveway was dirt. The car, driven by a teenage boy she had watched grow up, spun its tires as it backed onto the road. The car was lowered in the rear and had two chrome exhaust pipes extended past the bumper. In the car the boy's girlfriend sat so close to him they looked like one person. The car was loud. As it accelerated by, she read the false license plate mounted on the front. It said, "I LOVE COLD BEER AND HOT WOMEN."

"Boy's going to kill himself one of these days," Ervin said, startling her. "That girl sits so close to him there's no way he can drive safely," he said and started out the door.

"Where are you going?"

"To the hardware. To get a new lock set."

"I'm coming with you," she said. "Wait for me to get dressed."

She hurried. He was still there when she came out of her room. This gave her hope. She felt good riding off with him, doing something with him, being with him, even though he didn't say anything all the way there and back, at least they weren't fighting. It didn't feel as good as being sixteen and wrapped around your boyfriend, but it felt like something.

Ten

Three days before Christmas, Robert and Sally decided there was no way to get out of going to Wilmington.

"And Mother wants me to go to that special church service."

"I hope I don't have to go."

"You won't. Neither will Daddy."

"Great, I get to baby-sit for him."

The next day was the last working day before Christmas vacation. The other people in her shop were art students who worked part-time and were already gone. She had one project to finish and she didn't want to do that.

A salesman came in. He sold paper. She had been doing business with him for five years. He was a curious fellow. Some days he really came on strong, obviously interested in her. Other days, he was strictly legit. He was in his fifties. He was well preserved. He played tennis. He played golf. He had told her about all of this over the years.

"How about tennis sometime?" he asked.

"You know I don't play," she said.

"You don't play?" he asked, making a desperate run at a double entendre.

One of those days, she thought.

"No. Not tennis."

"I could teach you."

"I don't think so."

"Then how about lunch?"

"When?"

"Today. Now."

She was curious how far he would go. She was also curious how far she would let him go before she stopped him. She had just that morning made another list. It seemed to her, she had thought, that her life had revolved around men. This man or that man or the next one, or leaving the previous one and getting clear, and so forth. She made a list of the men she had slept with, and the list had thirty-seven names. This disturbed her, because she could not now imagine sleeping with anyone but Robert. It disturbed her that she had taken so long to settle down and had given so much and gotten so little for it.

Imagine, she thought, if she could get all of them together now, see them now, all in one room or, one at a time, bring them in for an interview, for observation, unseen, behind a two-way mirror, take a look at these fellows. Imagine, she had thought, how absolutely horrible it would be.

Thank God it was over, she had told herself when she closed her journal that morning.

"Sure. Lunch? Let's do it," she said.

"You look really good today," he said when they were seated. The Carolina Coffee Shop was full. Out of the corner of her eye she saw Adrian with a slim young man with one long, dangling earring.

"Thank you."

"You look fit, too. You don't play tennis, but you must work out some way."

"I don't play any sports. I work in the garden. I clean house. I walk from the car to the office. That's about it."

"That's not enough," he said. "You know all they say about the cardiovascular system these days."

"Maybe I should do something," she said. "But finding the time is so hard."

"There's always the weekend. Or after work."

She began to watch him as if she were watching a scene in which she was, and was not, a player, anticipating his next moves and her own.

"After work is out. I'm ready to go home then," she said.

"The weekends are always nice," he said. "I always keep my weekends free in case anything comes up."

They ordered. They ate. He kept on. He went further than she thought he would.

"Of course, there're other kinds of exercise."

"Like what?" she asked, pretty sure what he was going to say.

"Oh, I was just thinking," he said, and laughed, as if what he were going to say was funny, but a little naughty, giving her a chance to get ready for it.

"What was it?" she asked.

"I was just thinking about what Mae West used to say."

"And what was that?" she asked.

"About what kept her young. You know. Her love kept her young."

"Lovemaking, you mean?"

"Yes."

Now what? she thought.

"You know," he said, "I've known you all these years and yet I don't feel like I really know you. Know what I mean?"

Yes. I know exactly what you mean, she thought.

"You don't know me?" she said.

"Not the way I'd like to," he said as they sipped coffee. "Tell me about yourself," he said.

"There's nothing to tell. There's nothing to know. You tell me about yourself."

He did. He talked a long time. He talked through a coffee

refill. He wove, he thought, a perfect little web around her. He'd done it before.

"Now you tell me things," he said.

"My life's pretty dull," she said, and smiled at him. He fell for the smile.

"You know," he said, "you're a pretty woman. Everything about you. Especially your hair." He leaned across the table and looked closely at her hair. "I really love your hair."

This is it, she thought.

"I've always wanted to touch your hair," he said. "Do you mind?" he asked, and before she could answer, reached across and stroked it, letting his fingers caress her neck as he did.

She stared at him. She cocked her head sideways.

"Are you kidding me?" she said. "You just reached over and touched me."

"Well," he said, sitting upright and looking confused, "I thought . . ."

"You thought you could just reach over and touch me?"

"Well, see," he said, "it's just that, I thought that . . . well, I was just looking at you. . . ."

"And you thought what?" she asked, rather loudly, and he noticed people listening.

"Just calm down a second," he said quietly. "People are staring."

"Tell me what you thought," she said, louder than ever.

"I thought," he said, quieter than ever, "that it was going to be all right."

"Let me tell you something, mister," she said. "Don't you ever, ever touch me. I mean in any way," she said loudly, and stood up, knocking her chair over. He looked up at her, holding his hands out, palms upward, bewildered that his technique could have missed so badly.

"DO YOU HEAR ME?"

"I hear you," he whispered.

"No one but my husband touches me, you hear?"

He nodded.

"Just because I went out to lunch with you," she said, looking at him but talking to everyone in the restaurant who seemed unable, by any means, to exercise good manners and look away, "doesn't give you the right to touch my neck. You understand that?"

"I understand," he said, a bit more firmly, trying to gain control. "I made a mistake. Let it drop, how about it?"

"See that ring?" she asked, still standing over him. "You've got one, too. You want me to call your wife and tell her? You want that?"

No answer. She grabbed the edge of the table and tilted it to dump everything on his lap. He caught it. He steadied it. He pushed it back against her. They glared at each other while the coffee spilled and the cups slid around in their saucers.

"NEVER TOUCH ME AGAIN!" she screamed and then walked toward the door, leaving him in his chair looking as if someone had beaten him half to death, embarrassed, ruined and nowhere to hide. She walked on, and then, without planning it, looked at Adrian, who sat wide-eyed and open-mouthed with his thin friend whose earring wiggled as if he were shaking, and she stopped and said, "That goes for you, too, you little pimp," and she rushed on, having wiped out, in one locally historic minute of restaurant agony, in one historic minute of public horror, wiped out and destroyed one self-confident nervy man in love with himself, and a little weepy drag queen.

"You bitch," the earring guy squealed at her; only when he said "bitch," he pronounced it, bee-utch, and then he grabbed Adrian's hand and like lovers running not through the field of golden grain, but through the gauntlet of horrified disapproval and glaring disdain, pulled him into the bathroom, leaving the poor salesman to hide behind a cup of coffee, thinking, Boy, there's one fucked-up woman; but, of course, not daring to say it.

She walked up the alley beside the restaurant. The side of the restaurant was bricked up. There were no windows from which the diners could follow her and see what next she did.

Good, she thought. I'm glad I did that.

She went back to work. Would the salesman dare call again? she wondered as she sat at her light-table and fiddled with her T-square, sliding it up and down and feeling its smooth flow along its track.

Then, when she came home that evening, she told Robert about it and asked, "Now why did I do that? Really. It felt good to trap him like that, in there, and to embarrass him so badly, but then on the way home I thought, now why did I do that?"

"I don't know," he said. "But I'm glad you did. I don't want anybody messing with my baby but me."

"Still," she said, "I mean people flirt all the time. I mean, it just goes on."

"It better not."

"Not to that extent, but more subtly."

"I don't flirt."

"You look at other women."

"Not really. Maybe just a glance."

"I don't mind. I look at them, too. At men and women."

"I may have to kill that guy if he ever shows his face again."

"And that's the other thing," she said. "Unless he gets transferred, I'll still have to do business with him."

"I bet he'll stay on the other side of the desk."

"I imagine he will," she said, and walked out of the room and then stopped and came back and leaned against the door-jamb. "Still," she said, "it's so unlike me. It was just too perfect, I guess. It was so easy to trap him and he fell into it so fast, it just happened."

She leaned down and let her hair fall over, obscuring her face. She put both hands on her head and dug her fingernails into her scalp and scratched. "I've got to wash my hair tonight. We're going to Wilmington tomorrow. Remember?"

"How could I forget," he said.

"I'm so blue," she said on the way down. "I'm just worn out with these trips. I'm just worn out anyway."

"Maybe you're pregnant."

"Hey look," she said, "Don't joke about it. I can't take it, okay?"

"Sorry."

"I've got to figure out some way to break all of this."

"This what?"

"These trips, these parents, these things that enter my life over which I have no control."

"I saw something about that on the front of one of those magazines the other day."

"Look, I'm serious."

"I am too. Do you want me to turn around?"

"We can't do that."

"Sure we can. I just put my foot on this pedal and turn the wheel around and around."

"I know. I know. But we have to go through with it."

"That's what you always say."

"I don't know how to get loose. I don't know what I'm supposed to do. I hate being with them, but I feel sorry for them. I don't want to hurt them any more than they already hurt each other."

"It's up to you."

"It always was. I was always the peacemaker."

"Just do like I did," he said. "Just walk away and don't look back."

"I can't. I think about everything too much. About everyone. All the time."

"You're just too good."

"Right. I wish."

"Look," he said. "Let's pull in and eat before we get there."

"Good idea."

They pulled into the parking lot. The restaurant was in the middle of nowhere and was attached to a gas station which was attached by a chain link fence to a junkyard. They stopped the car. There were four other cars. Two men were standing in front of the cars and talking to each other. They poked and shoved each other playfully while they talked— salesmen, selling each other on something, so excited about being men they couldn't even remember what product it was they were selling that day, just talking and squeezing and pulling on their crotches and shifting around as if their shorts were caught up between their hips, and just having a time of it until Sally and Robert got out of the car and Sally walked around behind them wearing her long Guatemalan Indian dress and her huaraches and her long, fine and sparkling hair, so beautiful in the sunlight there with all its colors the world's best hair dye couldn't even come close, brown and blond and a little red here and there, all of it hanging down her back and the two men had to stop, these two men out in the world alone, their wives back home, stuffing in the food out of desperation and loneliness, and they had to take a look at this woman, they had to take her in as she walked by, drinking her in as she walked by, wanting her so much she felt it and she had to work to keep from staring back at these men who, it seemed, might never have seen a woman before in their life, but, like, holy shit, looky here, what's this, a woman, holy shit, and they watched her walk by and they shared her a little bit, looking back and forth and winking and thinking the same thing and letting each other know about it and all the time just getting more and more excited about being men.

"Creeps," Robert said once inside, and sat in a booth beside one of the rectangular plate-glass windows.

"What do you expect around here?"

"You couldn't pay me enough to live here."

"Nor me."

"I'm glad you left."

"I am too," she said, "or I might never have met you."

"Let's eat," he said and they ordered and ate and thoroughly enjoyed barbecue sandwiches and slaw and hush puppies and ice tea and chocolate pie for dessert and it was all real good. At least, they did raise good hogs around there.

They arrived in Wilmington in the middle of the afternoon. The temperature was in the fifties but another cold front was due. Robert parked the car in a way he hoped would discourage Ervin from noticing the damaged rear end and he took their suitcase from the back seat—he couldn't get the trunk open—and followed Sally and her mother to the backyard, where her father was at work.

"Steaks," he yelled, standing beside a massive red-brick outdoor grill.

Steaks? Robert thought, and he peered past Ervin to see if they were the same as usual. They were. They were thin, a half-inch thick, and were some of that same bargain meat he had bought a year ago, a whole cow and about fifty chickens and two dozen rancid pork chops and a long tube of bologna, all for about three hundred dollars, and the steaks were just unrecognizable, just totally unrecognizable in shape or cut, as if the cows had fallen off the truck and died on the way to market or been run over by a train; and tough, so tough it was like chewing steak-flavored parachute cloth, bloody and so stringy you ended up with threads of nylon stuck between your teeth or in your throat so that you went around for days afterwards hacking and coughing like a cat with a hairball.

"Steaks?" Robert whispered to Margaret. "Is that all he eats? Ever?"

"It was the war," she said. "He just didn't get any fresh meat over there for so long, so that ever since he's been back he's been crazy about steaks."

"I can't eat it," Robert later told Sally in her room, the same bedroom she had as a child. "I just can't."

"Try," she said.

"Oh. Try. Sure. Why not? It is Christmas. I guess I can gag down one more for him."

"You're sweet," she said, working hard to make everyone happy.

She later went to church with her mother while Robert excused himself and went to their room where he poked around in the drawers and in the closet, looking at mementos of his wife's childhood. He found a diary with the strap torn off. He looked through a stack of 45-rpm records. Dolls and magazines and books. It was like a museum. Everything had been preserved just as it had been when she left it.

"Yeah," Sally said later. "When I went to college, Mother said she was going to keep everything just as it was. She likes to live in the past, remember?"

"What about this diary?"

"Oh. Let me see it."

"There are some pages torn out."

"I know."

"How come?"

"Daddy. That was a big scene with Daddy. He found it one day, he didn't know I had one, and he read it."

"He read it?"

"He read it and I came in and found him reading it and grabbed it and ran into the bathroom and tore everything out and flushed it away."

"You mean he tore the lock off to read it?"

"Yes."

"I can't believe it."

"Things weren't too good back then, around that time."

"How old were you?"

"Fourteen, or so."

"What was inside?"

"Just the usual. I don't know how much he read."

"What did he do after you threw everything away?"

"Nothing. I don't remember. He was always messing around in my room, looking for things, trying to catch me."

"Doing what?" Robert asked.

"Smoking, anything."

"Smoking what?"

"Cigarettes, sweetheart. That's all we had back then."

"Right."

"Things happen, you know," she said, and began to undress for bed, "in families, and like, they must look awful, they must look weird and terrible to other people but for some reason, they make sense to the family involved. It's like, I mean, you look at your family, for instance."

"You can't compare mine to yours."

"No, but . . . ."

"I know what you mean," he said. "The private horrors of family life."

"Right."

"Now playing at your local theater."

"You got it," she said, and put on a robe and went to shower.

"It doesn't seem like Christmas," he said after the lights were out and they were in their separate beds.

"It's the weather," she said.

"I guess."

"What do you think they're going to give us?"

"I hope nothing."

"We could use money."

"I already saw three boxes in there. Yours, mine and ours."

"Uh oh."

"I'm beat," he said, suddenly exhausted.

"I'm not even sleepy," she said and a few minutes later, after a waking dream, she heard his regular breathing. "Goodnight," she said, but he didn't answer.

Later she turned toward him and felt in the air with her

hand. She stretched until she felt the edge of his bed and then inched her hand along until she touched his back.

"You want to come over here?" she whispered, far too quietly for him to hear.

The hall light shone under the bedroom door. The streetlight shone through the windows. They were steel casement windows, roll-out types, through which she had sneaked out many times. The metal was pitted from the salt air, but the cranking mechanism still worked smoothly.

She heard the muffled and strained conversation of her parents in the other room. For a moment, she felt excited and anxious as if she were a child and Santa were coming and she couldn't wait for morning. Only for a moment, though. She chewed on a fingernail and almost bit it off before she realized what she was doing. She stood at the window, looking at the empty street illuminated by the arc lights spaced every five or six houses.

Later, after falling asleep, she jerked awake at the sound of a door closing. She listened, then walked across the room and leaned toward the door, trying to discern who was up or what was happening. When she heard no more, she looked out the window again. A lone dog walked down the middle of the road, walking fast, as if he were late for something. After he walked out of sight, she remained where she was and pressed her lips and cheek against the cold glass. Then she heard walking again.

Ervin heard something, as well. He crept out of his room and down the hall. He stopped at Sally's room and listened. He held his breath and leaned toward the door with his fingertips against the wall for balance.

He started back to his room and heard movement again. He waited. He heard nothing.

They better not be doing it in my house, he thought. By God, they sure as hell better not be.

He stopped by his wife's room and listened to her through the closed door. She snored lightly.

Just like a man, he thought. She snores just like a man.

He went back to his room. He knocked down two more Unisom tablets and slept right through a throbbing hard-on that would have bothered the hell out of him had he been awake. He would have had to either do something with it, or not do something with it. Either way, it would have been hell.

Sally started on the fingernail again and then stopped and decided she was not going to sleep anytime soon and went into her closet, closed the door, turned on the light, and, for almost an hour, read through a stack of old *Seventeen* magazines. Then, at three, she went back to bed and slept until eight.

Eleven

The first day back at work Ervin took Angie out for lunch. He had missed her something awful.

"We're an item," she said.

"How's that?"

"People talk about us."

"Let them talk."

She had a salad. He had a steak and a baked potato. They were eating in the Western Sizzlin.

"But if enough people are talking," she said, "people who we don't want to know about us might find out."

"Don't worry about her," he said. "I'm going to fix that."

"How?"

"Don't worry about it. I just am."

"You know what people are saying?"

"Tell me," he said and took a big bite of steak. It was number six, the sirloin strip, and it came with Texas toast and baked potato or fries.

"That we're having an affair."

"But we're not."

"But people think we are."

"But we're not, so it doesn't matter."

She mixed the salad in her bowl. She had taken lettuce from the salad bar and then bacon bits, marinated green noodles, cherry tomatoes, mushrooms and chopped egg and grated cheese and topped it with French dressing. It was difficult to mix it without spilling and the cherry tomatoes rolled right out onto the table.

"Sorry," she said. She was trying to be so careful. She was also trying to stay slim. She'd been overweight for so many years that now, with her new life and a chance to start again with people who had never known her fat, she was determined to keep her weight down.

She was also being careful about how she handled Ervin. She liked him. More than she thought she would at first. He was gentle. He was courteous. He was slow. He was too slow, in fact. She was ready for more.

"My ex came up last night," she said.

"He did? What for?"

"To see Darlene. He came without calling. He's supposed to call. It's in the agreement."

"What happened? Did you let him in?"

"I had to. I didn't want a scene in front of Darlene."

"How long did he stay?"

"All night."

"I mean, what time did he finally leave?"

"And I mean," she said, "that he spent the night."

"Spent the night?" he asked and put his fork down with a piece of steak all ready to go.

"Uh huh," she said, looking down like a bad girl who'd been caught.

"But I thought, I mean, you know, I thought it was all over."

"I wish it were. It's so hard, being alone. You know what I mean? You're the only person I see. The only person I talk to."

"That's the way I want it," he said. "I want you to talk to me."

"You're nice."

"Now tell me all about it."

"I can't. I'm ashamed."

"Now you tell me, Angie. You tell me about it."

"Please don't make me."

"I need to know. I have to know."

"But why?"

"Because I do."

"Well, it was nothing," she said, and shifted her salad around, finally getting the tomatoes cut up without shooting the hard things off the bowl. "It was just something that happened. It got late. He was there. I was there. And then, it just happened."

Ervin had stuffed a giant bite into his mouth and he waved her to wait. When he got it chewed and swallowed, he said, "But that's not right. I don't blame you, but it seems as if he took advantage of you. He may have even come up just for that."

"He might have," she said. "He's like that."

"Then it's got to stop."

"I get so lonely, Ervin. I never go out at night. You're the only man I see," she told him again, and looked him right in the eyes. "I shouldn't have told you anything about it. Let's talk about something else." She was rather surprised how easily she had set the hook and how quickly he had bit.

"What do you want to talk about, then?"

"You," she said.

"Me? That's a boring story. You wouldn't want to hear that."

"But I would. I told you about me."

"Listen, if I were to dig down and tell you the story of my life you'd get up and run out the door."

"I would not."

"You would too."

"I most certainly would not. You underestimate me," she said and squeezed his arm. She squeezed hard. She dug her nails into his skin. She looked at him intently and smiled as she did. She dug her nails in until he stopped chewing and looked at his arm.

"You couldn't run me off that easily," she said, and dug a little deeper, quickly, a final jab that made him wince. After she let loose, there were four puncture marks in his skin.

"That hurt," he said. "You really hurt me."

"I meant to," she said, and speared a forkful of salad and put it in her mouth. The lettuce hadn't been cut up small enough. Part of a leaf hung from her lips. She stuck out her tongue and pulled it in. Seeing her tongue made him feel as if he'd seen her do something nasty. Between that and the red marks on his arm, he was so shook up he could barely work the rest of the day.

"Look at my arm," he said as she was getting out of the car at her apartment after work. "How'm I going to explain that to Margaret?"

"Keep your jacket on."

"But why did you do it? I don't understand."

"I did it because you don't understand. You really don't, you see, so I had to do something."

"What? What is it?"

"I like you Ervin. I don't know if it's your age or what, the difference in generations or what, but I've never," she said and moved so that her knees touched the side of his leg, "never, ever liked a man this much and not been further along. Do you get me now?" she asked, and she tilted her head around until she was leaning over him with her face next to his. "Do you get it?"

"Oh."

"Oh. Goodness sakes, Ervin. I like you, man. I've been sitting here telling you that and now what? Oh?"

"What?" he asked, actually bewildered.

"Is this a one-way thing?"

"No. I like you. I really do. I just didn't know, you understand, it's been so long. . . ."

"And, I know," she said, "I'm free and you're not."

"I guess that's it."

"I'm not being fair to you, am I, old man," she said and kissed him on the lips. His lips were dry and cracked and his breath was bad, but she hung in there.

"I don't know what to do," he said.

"You don't have to leave her, you know."

"But."

"Hey, listen Ervin, my big boy. I think this girl better slow down. This girl doesn't want to run off the only truly nice man she's ever known."

She pulled away.

"Do you really think I'm that nice?"

"Nice and good looking, too."

"Really?" he asked.

"Really. Now you know what you can do? Lean over and kiss me goodbye and think about it."

He did.

"By the way," she said, "Darlene's going to stay with her father this weekend." She closed the door. He watched her walk away. He drove home in a trance, as if he'd just seen an extraterrestrial being, which he had. He'd just had a close encounter with a passionate woman and it scared the hell out of him. By the time he got home he was ready to do better, to make up for being such a dolt.

But.

There she was, earthbound like a beached walrus in a chaise lounge, wrapped in a long coat with a blanket around her.

"I told you," she said, meeting him as he opened his door. He favored his arm as if it were broken.

"What now?"

"I told you about being late. Let me smell you," she said and stuck her head in the car and sniffed him.

"Get back," he said. "Get out of the way."

"I want to talk."

"Didn't you do enough of that the other night?"

"I want to talk and I want you to talk to me."

"I don't want to."

"But I do. I decided a few months ago that things were going to change, and they are."

"Talk to yourself, then. I've got to put some oil in the car."

"I don't want to talk to myself."

"Why? You do it all the time."

"So do you."

"I do not."

"You do so. I see your lips moving all the time."

"I'm singing if they are, or whistling to myself." He took a quart of oil from the shelf in the carport and opened the hood.

"If I talk to myself and you talk to yourself, maybe we should talk to each other more and we wouldn't be talking to ourselves."

"You lost me there, old girl," he said and punctured the can with a pouring spout.

"I want to talk about us."

"I know what you want to talk about," he said, mocking the sound of her voice, "but I don't."

"I want you to do this. I want you to tell me the things you don't like about me and I'll tell you the things I don't like about you. We'll make a contract, see, to change a certain number of things each way, to trade off, you know, get rid of some of my bad for some of yours."

"Where in the crap did you get that?" he asked, and laughed an ugly sneer at her and then pulled the breather from the valve cover, exposing the oil-filler hole. "Another one of those magazines? Give me a break," he said.

"What if I did? What's wrong with it?"

"What's wrong with it is you. You're what's wrong with it. There's nothing you can change about you that would interest me."

"Then why don't you leave me?"

"Is that an invitation?"

"No. But why, please tell me, please explain why you have stayed with me so long if you don't even like me?"

"Because you're too damn dumb to leave," he said.

"I'm serious," she said and pulled on his arm.

"Now look what you made me do. I spilled the oil on the alternator, you dumb bitch. Move out of the way and let me get a rag."

"I'm not in your way," she said.

"Just move," he said, trying to avoid being face to face with her.

"I will not move until you answer that question."

"I answered it," he said, sliding along the bumper to get out from between her and the car.

"Why don't you turn around and face me," she said. "You're scared to."

"Bull," he said and slipped free.

"You're a coward. That's what it is. You're scared to do anything. You're scared to talk to me, you're scared to leave me. That's it, isn't it?" she said, and nodded an affirmative to herself, as if in revelation.

"Listen, bitch," he said. "The day I'm scared of you is the day I cut my throat."

He walked onto the carport. He came back with one of his shirts.

"Don't use that," she said. "That's one of your good shirts."

"It's torn."

"I can sew it up."

"Forget it."

She reached for it. She got a grip on it. He held the other end.

"Give it to me."

"I will not. It's my shirt."

"But I can fix it."

"You can't fix anything," he said and walked off, dragging her.

"Quit pulling me."

"Let go of the shirt."

"I can sew it up. I used to sew them up for you."

"You used to do a lot of things," he said and jerked her forward and ripped the shirt half in two. She fell onto her hands and knees.

"Help me up."

He leaned into the engine and wiped up the oil. He put the breather cap back on. Without making a sound and moving so fast it surprised him, Margaret came up like a lineman charging forward at the snap of the ball. She grabbed him around his back. She pinned his arms to his sides and squeezed for all she was worth.

"What the hell?" he said, trying to look around to see how she had him. "Let go of me."

She held on. He fought to get loose. She was up on his back and she wrapped her legs around his and had his arms pinned with hers.

"Get off," he said.

He hopped toward the carport. He tried to get out of sight. She held on. She bounced up and down with him. Her legs were wrapped tightly around his so that her heels were inside his thighs. As he hopped, the spotlight from the garage that was trained on the driveway illuminated them in the dark yard.

"Come here quick," the next-door neighbor called to his wife as he stood at the window in a darkened room, watching.

"What is it?"

"Look. They're really at it this time."

"Oh my Lord," she said, and then let out a laughing sigh, kind of an "Ohooooooooo," but musical and high-pitched.

"What's she doing to him?" she asked.

"I can't tell. I'd just stepped in the room when I looked

out and she come up from the ground real fast and grabbed him around the back.''

''They are the oddest couple,'' she said.

''Always have been.''

''Look at his face,'' she said.

''She choking him.''

''It's about time.''

They jostled each other for a good position at the window, while outside, Ervin struggled on.

''Get off me. Let go.''

''I will not. I will not let go until you agree to talk with me.''

''Never,'' he said and hopped along toward the carport, panting and red-faced. ''Now you're choking me,'' he said in a strangled voice. ''I can't breathe.''

''I am not. I'm not even touching your throat.''

''I can't breathe, damnit,'' he moaned and looked to the carport to see how far he had to go to get out of sight.

It was forty feet from where she grabbed him to the carport. It was the longest forty feet of his life. It was longer than forty feet of North Korean hell.

He made it. He hopped around to the far side of the camper. He fell against it. His legs trembled. She weighed nearly as much as he did. As he fell against the camper, he wedged Margaret between him and its side.

''Now. Get off me.''

''If you will come inside and talk, I will.''

''Just get off.''

''Not until you say yes.''

''I can't think.''

''You think I don't know what you're doing, don't you?'' she asked.

''What? What do you mean?''

''Coming home late.''

''Listen,'' he said.

''You have a girlfriend.''

He slid onto his knees. She unwrapped her legs, but stayed on his back like a cowgirl resting on her stomach on a horse.

"Is that what this is all about?" he asked.

"I told you before. I told you long ago. If it's not going to be me, then it's not going to be anyone."

"You're crazy," he said.

"Not any more than you," she said, with her head resting on his back. He was still on his hands and knees. When he felt better, he crawled to the back door. She rode him upright holding on to his shirt at his shoulders and letting her feet slide along the concrete floor for balance.

"Who is she?" she asked.

He crawled to the steps. There were three steps. They were concrete like the carport floor. They led to the side door. He put one hand on the bottom step and said, "I can't get up with you on my back."

"Why are you going in?"

"So we can talk."

"I don't believe you."

"I've had it this time," he said, swaying from her weight as he rested one hand on the bottom step. "You win. Maybe it's time we worked something out."

"You promise? You swear to God?"

"I do. I'm worn out. I can't fight you anymore. Just get off."

She stood up and he crawled up the steps like a dog.

"Why are you crawling?" she asked. "Stand up."

"I can't. You've killed me. I can't walk."

He reached for the handle of the aluminum storm door and pulled it open. It had a strong closer and shut against him immediately.

"Will you hold this for me?"

"Sure," she said.

She stood on the floor to the side of the steps and held it wide while he crawled in. As soon as he got past the door, he whirled around and slammed the wooden entrance door in her face and locked it.

"Ha ha and double ha," he yelled at her. The door had three separate narrow pieces of glass in the top half. They were set at an angle, like stripes, all going the same way. He peered through one of these windows and pointed at her and laughed.

"I'll never talk with you, you damn crazy bitch," she heard him say. "Never, you hear?"

Then she heard him locking the other doors to the house and then she heard nothing. She sat on the steps. She began to cry. She cried quietly. Then she fell over. She fell over like the Buddhist monk in Vietnam who set himself on fire in front of the cameras and then burned, in a sitting position, until he fell over, still sitting, and still burning. She fell, still weeping, with her hands over her face and she lay on the dirty concrete slab without moving.

Later she heard him inside. The floor creaked as he walked back and forth. She heard the television. She heard the refrigerator open and close. She heard the water running in the pipes. She was cold. She wanted to call Sally. She needed to talk to her. She knocked on the door. She had been outside an hour.

He opened it. He turned his back on her. She went to her room. They did not say a word. She called her daughter. Ervin picked up the extension.

"I don't know what to do with him."

"But Mother, what can I do?"

"I don't know. What would you do if it were you?"

"I don't know. I can't imagine it. I can't imagine things going that far."

"It happens slowly," she said. "You hardly know it until it's too late."

"But it's never too late," Sally said and then hated herself for saying such a dumb thing. "I mean, people have options."

"What are they?"

"They can leave, they can seek counseling, things like that."

"I can't. Don't you see? I can't explain it."

"You don't have to. I've seen enough of it."

"But it's worse now. I really think he's got a girlfriend and though I always considered it a possibility, it hurts so much now that it's real."

"Can you talk to the minister?"

"I don't want anyone to know."

"That's it, isn't it?" Sally asked.

"What?"

"That you don't want anyone to know. It's pride."

"Is it? Is that what you call it?"

"I'm not helping you much, am I?"

"It helps to talk. To anyone. I guess I should go see someone. He won't talk to me and everything's all bottled up and confused inside."

"Write it down," she said. "Make a notebook of things, of thoughts, you know, like a diary."

"I've tried. I just don't seem to have the energy. I sit down and then can't think of anything to say."

"It's hard, I know. Listen, Mother, it's always worse before and after Christmas. You know you always feel better in spring. I don't know what to say. I don't know what to do. I feel for you, God knows I do, but I don't know what to say. I really don't."

They hung up. Ervin hung up. He heard Margaret in the bathroom. He quickly looked up Angie's number and called her. She did not answer. He looked it up again and dialed carefully. Still, however, there was no answer.

Margaret sat in her room on the side of the bed. It was late. She had eaten a tuna fish sandwich earlier and she kept burping up the smell. She gargled mouthwash and sat back on the bed. She stared at the carpet and began chewing on her finger. She worked her teeth under the nail and against the flesh and she rocked her finger back and forth against her teeth, not biting, just rocking, and she rocked herself into a trance, first on one finger, then another. She lay down. She couldn't sleep. She got up and went to the bathroom cabinet and took two codeine pills from a prescription left over from when she had back pain.

Soon she felt herself slipping, letting go, as if she were slowly dropping, dropping backwards, and as she dropped, the old unwelcome body tingled, sensuous again, and she drifted into a lonesome, sweet, delicious sleep.

As soon as Ervin heard nothing, absolutely nothing from her room, he called Sally. It was midnight. He woke her up.

"Daddy? What's wrong?"

"I just wanted to talk."

She knew, by the rules of the family, not to ask if he knew that Margaret had just called.

"Is something wrong?" she asked. She wore no clothes. She sat in the living room in the dark after lurching from the bed to the phone.

"Did I wake you?"

"I think so. Maybe I'd just fallen asleep."

"I'm sorry, baby," he said.

Baby? she thought. What the hell.

"What's going on down there?" she asked.

"I've got trouble with your mother."

"What is it?"

"I think she wants a divorce. She thinks I'm seeing someone."

"Are you?"

"Sort of."

"What does 'sort of' mean?"

"It means, I guess, that I am."

"Who is it?"

"Someone from work. A very sweet person."

"This is no good, Daddy. No good at all. I don't want to be in the middle of this."

"But you aren't. I just wanted to talk with you about it."

"But why now, Daddy? After all these years."

"I'm lonely, baby. I just am."

"But you said Mother wanted the divorce. That doesn't sound like Mother."

"Well, maybe we both do."

"Maybe you both better do nothing. Do you know how many years I've lived with your madness? Do you know?"

"I don't know what you mean."

"Of course you do. Let me tell you something. I'm worn out with it. I've got my own life. It takes all I've got to keep it going. I can't hold you two up any longer, don't you see?"

"But we never asked you. . . ."

"I've had to do it my whole life. One or the other of you has always come to me to figure out what to do with the other. You used to take me fishing and Mother used to take me shopping, or you used to go for a drive and then when I'm sitting there feeling great, come out with some crazy story about my very own mother, or she would do the same about you, and YOU KNOW IT," she screamed, and with that Robert rose out of bed as if he'd been electrocuted and ran into the living room.

"What is it?" he asked.

"Sorry," she said, covering the mouthpiece. "It's Daddy."

"Oh," he said.

"Get out of here," she said and waved him back.

"Are you there?" her father asked.

"Sorry, Daddy. It's late. I'm tired. I can't help you."

"I see I made a mistake calling you. I see my only child, my own daughter, doesn't want to help her father."

"It's not that. It's that I can't. I would if I could. But I can't."

"You're on your mother's side, I guess. You can't help it. You always have been."

"I'm not on anybody's side."

"You'd like her," he said.

"Who?"

"Angie."

"Angie. My God, is that her real name? Is she an angel?"

"In a way."

"This is too much."

"I'm going to try to get some time off to come up there and talk to you. Face to face."

"Don't do that."

"I'd like to bring Angie with me. I'd like you to meet her."

"Please don't do that. Just cool it for a while. Let's talk sometime again. Next week. And not at midnight, all right?"

After they hung up she stayed in the dark. She heard Robert breathing in the other room. She closed the bedroom door and then turned on a lamp. She walked through the kitchen. Two Christmas presents, a coffee-maker machine and an electric carving knife, were on the counter in a corner. She walked out onto the porch. The dog stood beside her.

She looked across the field. The house sat in a clearing. Back from the clearing, the dark woods shone in outline in the moonlight. The house itself glowed, a little bit the color of the yellow moon. The dog followed her into the field.

She stood in the cold field like a nymph, a jungle woman with long hair and perfect form, tight, sinewy, ready to run, an interloper who had come upon this house glowing in the moonlight and must decide to go back or go on, a woman without cover, in flight, her dog against her leg.

The civilized world lived in houses. Within the houses the most uncivilized things took place. Family members ate into each other. They cut each other up and then ate from the leftover torsos with forks, all the while ignoring the screams of the children who knew they were next. A moment there, in the early life of the family, in the sweet young beginning of parent and child, the charmed, precious existence of one to the other balanced and held true.

That moment gone, the doors shut tight, the windows locked, the blinds and curtains drawn, and the orgy of punishment and betrayal and deceit commenced. One day it was lollipops, the next day flesh, and the incestuous carnage surfaced like a dripping monster from the depths of the decaying family.

The next day, at school, at work, the smiling face of the shattered life hid, shamed into cover, and raced through the day, and then returned, having fooled the friends and lovers.

So she thought as she imagined the private terrorism occurring all over the world behind closed doors, as she imagined the shock of the friend, the lover, the fiancé, the husband, who then, fooled by the passionate desperation of the ravished heart, entered the family, too late to run.

And so, the next morning, she got up with Robert even though she wanted to sleep late, even though she needed to, and cooked his breakfast and petted him and cooed to him and made him late for work, all the while, as she lay on her back in the solid old bed, under his weight, all the while fighting the presence of other men.

The other men haunted her like recurring nightmares, the faces, the force, the suffocating dryness of their strange bodies like skin sloughed off and sucked in as she tried to breathe, she remembered, like not breathing at all, she thought, as her darling, cherished husband gasped quietly and breathed in, easily, clearly and happily, the vapors of his strangled wife.

Part II

The NIGHT
of the
WEEPING
WOMEN

Twelve

"Out with the old and in with the new," Margaret said early on the morning of January 2, as she passed Ervin coming out of his room.

"Ugh," he said and retreated.

She filled the water container and inserted it in the coffee machine. She knocked on his bedroom door. He didn't answer but she heard the shower and walked in. She knocked on the bathroom door, and then she opened it. He stepped from behind the curtain at the same time as she entered.

"Oh look at you," she said. "I'd almost forgotten what you looked like."

"Damn your ass," he said and covered up. "How'd you get in here?"

"The door was open. It looks like you put the knobs on backwards," she said and studied the arrangement. "The lock is on the outside."

"I don't give a damn where I put it."

"Well, it certainly doesn't matter to me," she said cheerily.

"What the hell is up with you? What are you so damn giddy about?"

"I'm going to start driving again."

"Sure you are."

111

"I want the keys to the Dodge."

"And if I give them to you, you're going to go out and—"

"Don't say it," she said, interrupting him, ". . . almost kill myself again."

"Right."

"That was a long time ago."

"And you haven't driven since you totaled that brand-new Chrysler, the best car we ever had."

"I'm ready now. It's a new year."

"You make me sick," he said.

"Just give me the keys."

"Your license has expired."

"I'm going to get a new one."

"You can't drive down there on an expired license," he said and then stopped himself as he flashed on the potential for another wreck, "unless you really want to. If you're set on it, take them. I'll drive the camper."

"You mean it?"

"Sure."

"Thanks," she said and leaned over to kiss him.

"Back off," he said.

She took the keys from beside his wallet on the night table and walked out; as she did, he entered the bedroom, still drying himself with the towel, and looked to see if she had separated the car keys from the others. Then he dressed and left. Margaret watched him out the window as she put on slacks and a blouse and a sweater and running shoes and a warm jacket.

I can do this, she thought. I steered it that time when he tried to kill me. Surely I can drive it by myself.

It was like riding a bicycle or skating. It came back to her. She drove slowly. She parked around the side of the license bureau. The lot was full. A notice on the door said sign in and wait. An old black man sat in a chair at the examiner's desk. His back was to the room. Margaret watched the old man. He was handsome and dignified and looked like an old darkie straight out of a Shirley Temple film.

"You don't have a license?" the examiner asked.

"No sir. That is why I am here," he said.

"Didn't I see you drive up in that car right there?" he asked and pointed to a big green car.

"Yes sir. You did."

"How can you be driving without a license?"

Margaret started to leave but just as she rose the examiner looked at her and said, "Just wait, ma'am, we'll get to you before long."

"You see, Mr. Offi-sir," the old man said, "I had my wallet stolen some time ago and the poe-lease man what stopped me inscructed me to come here."

There are people who just long for the good old days, they miss them something awful, but they keep quiet about it, having been instructed by the federal government to do so, but it had been a long time since an old-time nigra who knew how to talk to a white man had come into that license bureau and it just touched the examiner's heart, it did, it just took him back, and the old man could not have made a better case for himself if he'd tap danced and sang and clapped his hands, he could not have done any better if he'd come shuffling in and ast him if he's got any yards work, "Yes sir, I sure do's appreciates it," it was just hard to imagine how good it felt to find an old black who could make you remember the good old days, hell, you'd give him about anything just to come in and visit once a week, and it just touched the examiner deep inside, and he said, as softly and nicely as he could, "Well, if that's the case, Uncle Billy, I guess we will certainly let you have another license. Fill this out here. You can write, can't you?" he asked, hoping, God knows he was hoping Uncle Billy couldn't write so he could do it for him.

"I can write," the old man said, still dignified.

Margaret studied the book in her hand and worried about her own story. She had thought to read up right there and take the written test and then take the road test but now she had to worry about explaining how she got there and so she thought fast and said, when asked, "My husband drove me."

"And left the car here?"

"He rode to work with a friend who followed us over."

She had not lied in so long she was certain he could see right through her.

"And what if you don't pass?"

"Then I guess I will have to call him to come get the car," she said.

This was logical. He bought it. She passed and then waited while the laminating machine sealed her photo to the license and then she walked into the world, a registered mobile citizen once again.

All day Ervin laughed to himself, imagining the old woman in a wreck or in trouble for driving to the license bureau. It just made his day. He took Angie out for lunch again. He took her to a Chinese restaurant, the only one in town, and a place Margaret had always wanted to go.

"This is nice," she said as they were shown into a booth with a curtain that the host drew, sealing them off in their own world.

"You're nice to take me to lunch so often. You must let me take you out sometime."

"Wouldn't think of it," he said, studying the menu.

"Buddy wouldn't even take me out, not after a while. He did at first, but then, I don't know, after Darlene was born, he just wouldn't go anywhere with me."

"Wonder why?"

"I never could figure it out."

"I know what you mean," he said, a bit distractedly, as he studied the menu, lost once he left steak and potatoes.

"You order for me," he said. "I trust you."

"Anything? Do you like anything, really?"

"Don't get me any squid or octopus or anything like that."

"Moo shoo pork is good," she said. "We can order extra pancakes and share it. And some Chinese wine?"

When it came, she prepared the pancakes with the sauce and the filling and set them, one at a time, as he ate, on the extra plate they had asked for. After he finished two, she fed him a third, reaching across the table and putting it right in his mouth.

"I'm glad that curtain's drawn," he said.

"You're just an old prude."

"I am. I am old. You ought to know that."

You're just right, she thought, imagining quiet nights and a fatherly warmth, not to mention a thirty-year civil service pension. "Even if you retire like you said you were going to, you're so healthy and young-looking you could do anything else you wanted."

"You paid for your lunch with that," he said.

She slid forward and her knee touched his knee and then, relaxed and feeling so comfortable in their private booth, she slid a bit further, straddling his leg with both of hers.

"I like you," she said, sleepily, dreamily, warmed up by the wine and the closeness. "It's so hard sometimes being alone. Of course, I'm not alone, but I mean with Darlene, all the time. I love her. I don't mean I don't, and I wouldn't take anything for her, but it gets so tiring. I had an awful fight with her the other night. It was one of those days, you know, when she felt bad and I felt bad and she was just on me, all day. She never let up."

"That's bad."

"You know what I mean. You have a daughter. You remember those days when you can't stand another minute in the house with them, but then, if you leave, you can hardly wait to come back. It's kind of like that. A person needs something else."

"That's for sure."

"I like you because you pay attention to me. Because there's something there, the way we are together, that I've missed. I didn't think I'd miss it, not after all I went through, but I have."

"I miss it, too."

"Buddy was very selfish. He didn't mean to be, I don't even think he was aware of it. It was just the way he was. On certain nights he would be nice to me. Just a little. For just a little while, he would pay attention to me, and then, after I gave in, nothing," she said, and opened her palms to show what she meant. "Nothing, that is, until the next time. It was awful."

Ervin listened. The glass of wine was the first alcohol he'd had since he was in the army. He felt so different from any way he had felt in so many years he knew more clearly than ever before how much he wanted out and how much he wanted this sweet, lonely young woman.

"It's bitterness," he said.

"What?"

"Your husband was probably bitter."

"My ex, please. But about what?"

"Oh, I don't know. Something must have happened that put a bad taste in his mouth and he couldn't get rid of it."

"Why do you say that?"

"Just a guess."

"Is that what happened to you. With your wife?"

"Maybe."

"What was it, then?" she asked.

"Nothing. Or, well, I mean, everything, really. It wouldn't do any good to talk about it."

"But I want to know."

"Well, it's like she lives in a dream world. Of course, now that I hear myself saying it, it doesn't sound so bad."

"What's it like?"

"What's it like? Well, for instance, when I go home, I never know what to expect. She's all over the map. She's fine one day, calm and leaves me alone, and the next day, out of the blue, she's like a crazy woman. Chases me around the house. All kinds of things."

"That's awful."

"I don't know why I married her. I can't remember now. But anyway, I shouldn't be talking about it. It's not your problem. It's mine."

"Maybe it's ours."

"No. I wouldn't do that to you. There's no reason you should believe me, anyway. I might be making it all up. It might be me who's the crazy one."

"I doubt that," she said.

They lost track of time so that later they had to rush to get back to work and Angie, running out with him, saw them reflected in the big window of the camper as they ran toward it.

"We look nice together," she said. "Don't you think?"

"I do."

"Why did you bring this, anyway?"

"Margaret took the car."

"Oh. I thought you said . . ."

"She's got her license back. Or, she was going to get it. The new year and all. She's always starting some new plan, always has some new idea. Big changes. All the time," he said, and made a grim face.

"One thing I always wanted to ask you," she said, thinking about the car.

"What's that?"

"Why'd you act like your window wouldn't roll down that first time I rode with you?"

"When was that?"

"After I took my car to the mechanic. When you were sitting there at the store and I knocked on the window?"

"Oh yeah. Right. That was when, well, it wouldn't then. I got it fixed."

"You acted like you didn't want to give me a ride. I thought, you know, before I asked you, when I walked up to you, that you'd be glad to give me one. You'd been staring at me for weeks.''

"I had not."

"You had too," she said. "You just stared at me like I was the first woman you'd ever seen, or something. I didn't know what to make of it at first."

"I must have been smitten," he said.

"Now we both are," she said, and they drove off.

Margaret was home by one-thirty, in time to see her favorite soap. She shopped after she left the license bureau and took herself out to lunch. She had spent more than two hundred dollars.

"Don't pick me up this Sunday," she told Evelyn, her friend who took her to church.

"Are you going out of town again?"

"I've got my license."

After the soaps she went into her bathroom, and in one of the more courageous moments of recent life, dragged the scale from under the sink and actually stepped on it.

"Oh my God," she said out loud. "I never."

At four-thirty she watched an afternoon talk show, and as if God had heard her calling from the bathroom, listened to a man describing a new diet.

I'll do it, she thought. And I'll put Ervin on it, too.

Then, checking the refrigerator and the freezer and failing to find anything that strictly conformed to the new ultra-low-carbo plan, she drove to the grocery store and bought what she needed. Ervin would be home in a little more than an hour.

About the time Margaret checked on the chicken and tossed a light salad of lettuce and carrot strips, Ervin and Angie climbed into the camper.

"She went to get her license," he explained as he started off, "because it is a new year."

"A time for new beginnings, of course."

"But she shouldn't try it. She can't drive very well."

"I see," Angie said. She was eager for any kind of information on the wife.

"Anyway, that's neither here nor there."

"If you say so."

"I wish I didn't have to go home."

"I do too."

"But what can I do?"

"It's difficult," she said.

"It's not your problem, though. I shouldn't drag you into it."

"I am in it, though. In the middle, you might say."

"I hate that," he said.

"Don't hate things," she said. "It's not good for you."

They drove quietly along. Ervin took the long way home down Front Street, where previously declining grand houses now stood renovated, the Cape Fear River flowing behind them and, in the distance, across the shore, the battleship *North Carolina*, open to the public and, during the season, lighting the skies with its reenactments of battles at sea.

"I love these houses," she said.

"They're nice."

"I wish you didn't have bucket seats."

"These are captain's chairs," he said. "They're not exactly bucket seats."

"But I can't sit close to you this way."

"Oh," he said looking at her.

"I like to be close. If you haven't guessed."

"I have a daughter your age," he said.

"I know that. I don't care."

"She might even be older."

"So what? People are ageless in certain ways."

"Such as?" he asked, looking in the rearview mirror as a car behind them illuminated his lined face.

"Such as in kindness, in generosity, in warmth, in love. Such as," she said, "in those things."

"It's been a long time," he said.

"For what?"

"For anything. For any of those things you just mentioned."

"Maybe you were saving it."

"Maybe so," he said, and drove on without speaking, all the way to the Brookstone.

"Where's Darlene?"

"Upstairs, I suppose. Why?"

"What if you were a little late?"

"It wouldn't matter. Mrs. Scholtz will stay until I get there. She knows to."

"Do you want to just sit here and talk?" he asked.

"I thought you'd never ask," she said, and climbed through the passageway between the seats and settled down on the bench along one side.

"Back there?"

"Why not. You've got a traveling home here. It's nicer than my apartment."

"Oh, it's not."

"It is. I could live here."

"Some people do. They put them up on blocks," he said as he joined her, "and hook into utilities and have a little house."

"Why not?"

"I can turn a light on, if you want."

"We don't need it. The light coming through the windows is just right."

"I don't know what to do, you know."

"Sit closer to me, for a start," she said, and he moved against her and she lay her head against his shoulder, snuggling under his arm. He sighed. Her closeness slowly worked through him, and with the sigh he lay his head against hers and breathed in the sweet smell of her hair, her neck, her skin.

At five forty-five, Ervin was fifteen minutes late. Margaret took out the chicken and unwrapped it, stuck it with the meat thermometer and watched the needle rise and then pushed it back in the oven and closed the door, turning the dial to the lowest setting of warm and left the kitchen.

She went into his room and searched through his drawers. She searched them neatly and methodically and looked in his closet and behind his clothes and in the dark corners and on the half-shelf above the rod. She looked for evidence and she found in his night-table drawer an updated list of post office employees. She knew all the names but two. She wrote their names and addresses on a piece of paper and got in the car, a licensed investigator now, and went to find her husband.

The first address was beside the name Chandra Alston and was in a part of town she knew little about and when she saw through the lighted windows the family inside and no camper in sight, she backed out and started for the Brookstone Apartments to find out about this other name, this Angela Taylor.

The address was across town and would take fifteen minutes to get there.

It began to rain and from inside the camper Ervin remembered sleeping under the tin roof of his parents' farmhouse.

"It's raining," he said.

"I know it is. I like the rain."

"It's cold, though."

"Let's get a blanket around us, then," she said.

"I mean outside. It must be in the thirties. The temperature's been dropping all day."

"So?"

"It might freeze."

"Good," she said.

"I mean onto the roads," he said.

"That'll be just right, won't it, baby," she said.

"Do you think," he said, "I mean, do you want . . ."

"Yes."

Cars driving in and out of the parking lot swept the camper with their lights, searchlights on this couple inside the thin walls, kissing hard enough to make lips bleed.

"Take it easy," she said.

"I'm sorry. I don't know what I'm doing."

"Don't move. Just stay just like that. Let me."

He shifted while she was kissing him; he reached toward the window.

"What's the matter?"

"I want to close the curtains."

"Are the doors locked?" she asked.

"No."

"Then lock them."

"What about Darlene?"

"Don't worry about her."

He made the bench into a bed, a narrow single bed on which they entwined like snakes.

"I never . . ." he said.

"Never what?"

"Never thought I'd feel this way again."

"Do you like it?"

"I think so."

"Do you want to get undressed?"

"Do you?" he asked.

"Yes. Do you have another blanket?"

He got the blanket from the storage chest above the bed. The blanket was old and was from a double bed from long ago.

"Nice," Angie said.

They snuggled, still dressed, under the blanket and she pulled him over on top of her. She held him against her with her arms and her legs and she pressed against him so hard he couldn't move or think, he just held on and tried to stay with her.

"Let's take our clothes off," she said.

"Where?"

"Anywhere you want," she said and took hers off right then and there, proud of her new figure and showing it off for the first time since she had begun eating what must have been by that time a tractor-trailer load of lettuce and celery and carrots.

"You like me?"

"I like you," he said, and she slid under the covers.

"Now you."

"Okay," he said and looked toward the doors and the windows.

"No one can get in, can they?" she asked.

"No. I don't think so."

"Then come on baby. I've been waiting a long time for this."

He thought about his old-man body and his skinny little ankles and the bald places on his legs where the hair had fallen off and he thought about that little thing inside his pants and would it look right, I mean, did the men these days, I mean, he thought, was it the same? and he said, "I think I'll get undressed under the covers," and he climbed in with her and took off his shirt and as it came off she reached for him.

"You're shy," she said.

"Not for long," he said, and kicked until he got his pants off and then his boxer shorts and as soon as he had them off she reached for him, there, too.

"Whew," he gasped.

"Are my hands cold?" she asked, and put them to her lips.

"No. This stuff is a little new to me."

"You mean?"

"I mean."

"How long?"

"Oh, I don't know. Just not too often, is what I mean."

"Well we'll change that," she said. "You bring that little boy over here and I'm going to make him into a big boy," she said and went to work. She worked hard, there's no denying it, and she did everything just right. After all she'd had years of experience with her drunk-soldier husband, a recon man who could drop from a rope down the side of a mountain or free fall with a parachute until he was three thousand feet up and pop that cord and hit the target dead on, lots of experience, you see, even when dead drunk and still wanting it, she could get him there, the quicker the better, too, so they could go on to sleep, and so she knew just what to do.

"That's nice," he said.

"Just relax. Think about what you're going to do to me."

And still nothing was happening, like the nothing that would happen if you took some cold hamburger meat and sculpted it just so and then tried to force it into a steaming-hot slab of rump roast just out of the oven, that kind of nothing, about that firm, you see, like that cold pop-art penis, nothing, you see, nothing, when, had Ervin known it, he could have done anything to her, just anything, so much she wanted to be his at that moment, so close she was to having him just where she wanted him, she would have said yes to anything, to whatever he needed, baby, you know, I just want to, I just need to, you see, take this knife and slice your belly open a little, not too much, but just a little, all right, all right, just take me, just do with me, turn me over and do with me, stand me up and do with me, push me down and do with me, I'm yours, she had told him, but he just didn't know what it meant and there was still that cold piece of hamburger down there, and every time she reached for it, it practically disappeared, talk about something slipping out of your grasp, just gone, like that, and in its place in that tortured guilty mind sending the signals across synapses that hadn't seen a twitch in years, in its place a soft, fleshy statue of Margaret Neal appeared, like a pale, white bat she hung there upside down, staring back at him.

Angie was having her own troubles keeping her mind on things by then, thinking, there goes that thirty-year pension, there go the warm nights by the fire in the new condominium she had looked at one Sunday afternoon, just dreaming, just planning ahead, and here come more of those endless days in the post office walking on the concrete floor until the bones in her heels had pounded up into her brain, all of that not quite so distinctly, but she knew she was losing her momentum.

"You bitch," he said.

"What? Did you just call me a bitch?" Angie asked, sitting up.

"No. I certainly did not."

"You did. I heard you."

"Oh. I guess I was thinking of Margaret."

"But don't do that. Think about me."

"I want to. Believe me," he said, stalling for time and trying to find some way out of this humiliation, trying to find someone, anywhere, and who better to blame than the nemesis of his life, that queen of the housecoat and terrycloth slippers, that woman who knew way, way, way too much about him, knew so much he couldn't ever get past it all, so he thought it was time, it was time like no other time would be, to tell Angie one of the reasons he couldn't leave the poor old girl and why this saint of a man couldn't betray her.

"She's crippled," he said, and Angie asked, "What? Who?" and he said again, "I just didn't want to tell you but I guess you need to know."

"You mean Margaret?"

"Yes. One of her legs is crippled and she has to wear a brace on it. I didn't want to say anything. I've tried to protect her. But you need to know."

"Oh, I'm so sorry."

"And every time I get fed up with her and try to leave

her," he said, seeing it as he said it, "I just look at that leg and that brace and watch her clunk across the room and I just sit back down and I can't get any further than that, you know, like tonight, I just can't. I just don't know how I'll ever get away from her."

"Come here, honey," she said and held him against her. "I had no idea. I really didn't," and she began to see what he had been through, all that he had been keeping inside himself and she held him and rubbed his hair and rested against his shoulder even though his armpits smelled like the inside of an old shoe, she gave what she could, both of them silent while they tried to figure out what next to say, what next to do, where, just exactly, they could go from here, both still and so quiet that when something bumped against the outside of the camper, they jumped like one person.

"Ervin," the thing that bumped called. "Ervin, are you in there?"

"Oh God," he whispered. "It's her."

"Margaret?" Angie whispered.

"Yes."

"Are you sure?"

"Ervin?" she called again and tried the door.

They dressed and put away the blankets and folded up the bed, all the while staying below the level of the windows.

"I can hear you in there, Ervin Neal. You open up right now."

"Get down," he said to Angie, who was on the floor.

"I am down."

"I hear voices," Margaret called. "What are you doing? Who's with you in there?"

She pulled on the door again. He remembered the bathroom door. He stepped over Angie and started the engine and drove off as fast as he could, bouncing over the curb and into the street while Angie rolled around like an empty pop bottle and Margaret stood in the rain for a moment and then started after him.

"Take it easy," Angie said.

"Stay down. She's coming after us."

"Lose her."

"I can't."

He cut in front of a line of cars and turned right. The cars slammed on brakes in chain reaction. Margaret was trapped behind them trying to get out of the driveway.

"That car's got a four-barrel carburetor and a high-performance cam," he said, "and we'll never outrun her."

He drove around the block and ran a red light and stopped behind the apartment complex in the shadow of the buildings.

"Jump out," he said. "Out the back."

She leaped and he started off before she closed the door and it swung back and forth, and by the time Angie disappeared around the building and he turned the corner, Margaret caught up with him. She saw him as the door swung open. Her headlights lit up the inside of the camper and the back of Ervin's head and she could see his eyes reflected in the rearview mirror. Ervin hit his brakes but then quickly let off and the forward impact slammed the door shut as Margaret slid toward him on the wet street. He floored it and pulled away, but she caught him again and followed him, this time from a distance, all the way home.

"This is it, Ervin Neal," she said after they were both out.

"What? What's it? I didn't do anything."

"I know what you're doing. I know her name. Now where is she?" she asked and pushed by him to search the camper.

"You're making a fool of yourself," he said. "As usual."

"Don't lie to me. I'm sick of it."

"Be sick of it, then."

"Where is Angela?"

"Who?" he asked, amazed she knew her name.

"Angela Taylor, your girlfriend from the post office."

He walked to the house and she followed him. He walked

in front of her in the blind terror a person felt on the sidewalk after sensing that someone had walked up close behind him and he was about to be mugged. Afraid, but more afraid to turn around and face it. When they were in the carport, she struck.

"Hey. Calm down. All right?" He had fallen against the storm door and knocked the Plexiglas panels out. "Look what you did now. You're tearing things up again."

"I'll tear you up if you don't tell me what's been going on."

"Okay. You've got me. Come on in and we'll talk."

"You mean you were with her?"

"Yes."

"You mean you admit you've been seeing her?"

"Yes," he said and she followed him into his room.

"And have you?"

"Have I?"

"Have you and her?"

"No. We haven't done that."

"You better not have."

"Don't worry."

"Don't worry, you say," and made as if to hit him again when suddenly she just dropped, lifeless, like a puppet whose strings had been cut all at once and she wept and she wept in such a deep, moaning way and with such force that Ervin, in spite of everything, felt sorry for her and he sat on the floor and held her.

"You don't have to," she said.

He held her with his arm around her shoulder and supported her until she stopped heaving and shaking and she looked up at him and he looked down at her and it was the perfect moment to kiss, to forgive, to make up, a scene from a movie, come true. It was six-thirty. Forty-five minutes had passed since the chicken went back in the oven to stay warm. Outside it was still raining, the temperature was still falling and was, at that moment, thirty-eight degrees.

* * *

At seven, raining harder in Chatham County than on the coast since the rain and the cold were coming from the northwest, Sally told Robert that supper would be delayed still more.

"It'll be worth waiting for," she said.

"I don't mind."

"It's the cheesecake."

"I can wait for that."

"We could eat now and then wait on dessert."

"Let's do it right. I'll take a bath."

"Okay."

"I'll light the gas heater."

"We've got to get some more wood in, as well."

"I'll get that later."

Sally's journal was on the clothes hamper where she had left it that morning. Robert picked it up. He didn't know about the journal since she only wrote in it in the mornings after he left.

What's this?

He read the open page. It read like the kind of nonsense he wouldn't read if he found it in a women's magazine but because it was his wife's nonsense, he read further and then flipped back to the beginning. The title had been written and erased a number of times. It now said, "Journal of My Flights."

What flights?

While he was reading he had the sense he should not be, but he continued on.

Just curious.

He filled the tub. He stayed in the water until it turned cold and then stood in front of the open, fire-bricked gas heater and dried off. He heard the floor creaking and put the book down and dropped his towel over it.

"It's ready now," Sally said, leaning in.

"Just a minute more."

"Did you fall asleep?"

"No. Why?"

"You've been in here half an hour."

"Just give me a minute to get dressed."

The kitchen table was arranged as if for a photograph. There was ambrosia and roast duck and wild rice and snap beans and sautéed mushrooms and, in the refrigerator, the cheesecake with blueberry topping.

"This is a kind of midwinter present," she said. "Twelfth Night, Russian Christmas, or what have you. Anyway," she said, "you've been so good putting up with Mother and Daddy and all the visits and the rubbery steak, I just thought I'd do it."

"Looks great," he said.

"Aren't you hungry? Let's eat."

"You left a book in the bathroom."

"What book?"

"The journal of your flights."

"Oh. That book. Well, thanks. Where is it?"

"Still in there."

"I'll get it later."

"I read it," he said. "I'm sorry, but I did."

"You shouldn't have done that. I wouldn't read something of yours I saw was personal. Not without asking."

"I know."

"Why didn't you ask me?"

"I don't know."

"So. What do you want me to say?"

"I want to know if it's true."

"Maybe and maybe not."

"Because if it is, something strange has happened. Because if it is, then you're not the person I thought you were. If all that stuff is true, then I don't even know you."

"That's ridiculous," she said, and tried to keep on eating.

"It really is. I'm the same no matter what."

"But you're not."

"But I am."

"But, thirty-seven men. Really?"

"Oh hell. That would be the part you found," she said.

"Can that be true? I mean, you've got their initials down there, and dates, I mean, what in the hell? How could you do that? How could anyone sleep with that many different people? I mean, you'd almost have to be crazy."

"Not crazy," she said, embarrassed and humiliated. "Not crazy, exactly, but kind of desperate."

"Either way, it makes me wonder."

"Me, too. That's why I wrote it down."

"Come in here," he said and took her by the arm and guided her from her chair and the perfect meal and into the other room, while back at the table the ambrosia curdled.

It was the perfect moment to be kissed, there on the floor with the tear-streaked face and the broken heart and the protective arm of Ervin around her, but it passed, without the kiss.

It passed without the kiss because hard as he tried, much as he hated to see her hurt that badly, much as he hated her for so many things and as much as he wished he hadn't done or said so many of the things he'd done or said, he had to let the moment pass, because he had, during that moment, decided he needed Angie in his life and that he would be able, finally, to leave this worn-out old woman.

It was so important not to make mistakes with the person you loved, and there were so many mistakes already made with Margaret there was no way out of them.

"Wash up," he said.

"Why?"

"Just go wash up," he said and led her into the bathroom. "I'll get you a clean towel."

She filled the bowl with cold water. She cupped her hands and splashed it on her face. She heard the door close and found herself alone in the room.

"Ervin?"

"Sorry," he said.

"What?"

"I've got to do some things. I just can't have you interfering."

She pulled on the door but it was locked and when she reached to unlock it, looking for the button one would find in any bathroom-door lock, she found nothing. Yet, the door was still locked.

"Open up, now. This isn't funny."

"I know it's not."

"Where's the lock button?" she asked.

"It's on the outside. Remember? I put the knobs on backwards," he said, changing clothes, "and when I did it I thought I'd just change them around later. I see now," he said on his way out the bedroom door, "that there was a purpose to it."

She heard the bedroom door close. She heard him drive off and she sat on the closed top of the toilet seat with the green and purple cotton cover that matched the green and purple oval rug on the tile floor and she looked in the tub and saw a mass of hair caught on the drain guard and without knowing she was doing it, scoured it clean with her fingers and tossed the hair into the trash.

"Really," Robert said, "what does that make me? I mean, think about it. You know what it makes me? Number thirty-eight. That's what it makes me. Number thirty-eight."

"Of course it doesn't."

"I mean, you know, we don't expect our wives to be virgins nowadays, but then again," he said, and thought back, "then again, that explains why you are such an expert in bed. That explains a lot."

"It doesn't explain anything," she said.

"It explains how you know so much and what a damn fool I've been. I must have looked like a real jerk to you. Imagine how you've had to teach me everything. Goddamnit. That makes me feel like a real fool. I mean, you know, like I said, we don't expect our wives to be virgins, but then again, we don't expect them to have been professionals in the business, either.''

The cat walked in. He walked toward Robert. The dog knew better and hid behind a chair but the cat walked right up and rubbed against his leg and got kicked across the room.

''Goddamn cat.''

''Don't.''

''Don't? Shit,'' he said, and then he said it three more times. ''Shit, shit, shit.''

''That's nice,'' she said. ''That's really intelligent.''

''Oh, you want to get tough?''

''No. I don't want to get tough. I just want it to be over.''

''Then tell me about it.''

''I don't want to do that.''

''That's the only way it'll be over.''

''Can't you see how embarrassing this is for me?''

''And can't you see what it makes me?''

''No. I can't.''

''It makes me number thirty-eight.''

''Don't say that again. Really. It's meaningless.''

''Somehow it's not.''

''But it is.''

''Just tell me.''

''You really want me to?''

''I do.''

''But where do I start?''

''At the beginning.''

''Let's eat first. At least let's do that.''

''I'm not hungry.''

''This is so strange,'' she said. ''I ought to just go eat my supper and forget all about this.''

''But you can't, because you know you're in the wrong.

You've deceived me. You've betrayed me. I thought you were mine, but now I find out you were everybody's."

Ervin rang Angie's doorbell, and Mrs. Scholtz came out from next door.

"Are they home?" he asked. "Do you know?"

"They're not home. They left a few minutes ago."

"Exactly how long ago?"

"I don't know. Not exactly."

"Where'd they go?"

"I don't know that either. I just saw them get into her old car and leave."

"But that car won't run."

"It runs a little."

"Have you got a key you could let me in to wait for them?" he asked.

"I couldn't do that."

"Yes you could."

"No. I don't think I could," she said and closed her door and would not answer when he rang her bell.

"You tell her I have to talk with her," he yelled through the door. "Tell her it's important."

He drove to the nearest FastFare and bought a large cup of coffee and a box of Krispy Kreme doughnuts.

Meanwhile, Margaret had already tried the doorknob with force, hoping to tear it off, but it held. She pushed against the door with her shoulder the way police broke down doors on television but it would not open.

"Let me out," she said to no one but herself.

She beat on the wall. There was a wall adjacent to the hall, one adjacent to her bedroom, one adjacent to his bedroom and one on the outside wall. There was sheetrock, insulation, blackboard and four inches of brick between her and the outside world. She yelled. Her voice was faint and a person would have to have been standing directly outside the wall to hear her.

* * *

"I was not everybody's," Sally said. "I have never been anyone's but yours."

"Sure."

"You don't understand it. You should, but you don't. I can see that. I have been loyal to you, so fiercely loyal to you. No one," she said, "was ever as loyal to a husband as I have been to you and it's because everything's so right between us."

"Was so right," he said.

"You just don't know. You just can't know, I guess, you just can't understand, I guess, unless you know what I've been through and what I've had to live with. I guess that's the way it's going to be. I'm surprised you haven't asked about that, too?"

"What?"

"If you're asking what, then I guess you haven't read the whole journal. I guess if you had, you probably wouldn't be here by now."

"What else is there?"

"Listen. If I tell you all this sordid stuff and we talk about it, will it be over? Can we just let it go?"

"I guess so. I don't know. But maybe."

"See, you wondered why it's been so hard on me that I haven't been able to get pregnant, why I went through that stupid arthroscopic surgery and all that. And, of course," she said, "Daddy figures into this."

"It's getting worse all the time, then," he said.

"He just has made such a mess of things. I don't know how he could do it. With Mother and with me. He just has done all the wrong things."

"I'm listening," he said, trying to close off any expression on his face and have that dead look the therapist had when the patient looked up and said, "But listen, you see, I've killed sixteen people, eaten little children for breakfast, fried them in a pan, I killed the Pope and ate his toes and there's nothing better I like than a real good thick shit sandwich,'' and the therapist just sat there and nodded, as if, ''Of course, of course you did all those things,'' he sat there like that, waiting for whatever it was.

''Well,'' she said. ''Talk to me. Say something,'' she said and reached for him and he pulled away.

''Don't touch me right now. My skin feels crazy. I can sit here but don't touch me.''

''But baby,'' she said, ''I want to be sure this is the right thing. I want to be sure we are closer, not further apart after all this is over. Don't leave me now.''

''I'm right here. Just go on.''

''Well, I was fourteen—'' she began.

''Fourteen?'' he cut in. ''You were fourteen when you started?''

''Just listen to me, please. I was fourteen and we were living in Wilmington in that same house, and Mother and Daddy were fairly normal, still slept in the same room, I think, I'm not sure, anyway, they fussed and fought a lot but at the time I thought it was just the way things were, not knowing life could really be any different, hoping it would or could be, but not really sure.

''Anyway, that year things went bad for them, I don't know why, and Mother wrecked the car that year and quit driving, and they started fighting more and I started hating it so much all I could think of was getting out and getting away, graduating, having my own life, just anything but staying with them.

''So naturally, there I was, ripe for some nice boy to come along and just do with me anything he wanted and that's what happened. I got this crush on an older boy, who was in the eleventh grade, and this led to that and so on and pretty soon we were sleeping together.''

''At fourteen,'' Robert said, and shook his head. ''A baby.''

''I wasn't a baby. I was mature, but it was early. It really was. I think I was the first girl in my group of friends to do it. But you know, it wasn't like really making love. It was more like, I don't know, more like speeding in a car or sneaking out. It felt the same. A kind of rush. A kind of illicit thrill. It was not," she said and reached over and touched him on the back of his hand, which he pulled slowly away, "it was not," she said, "like what we do. Nothing was ever like that. You have to know that. Nothing was ever like that. It wasn't making love. It was more like the thrill of doing something wrong."

"I bet."

"And," she said, ignoring the remark, "I had that diary, the one you found with the pages torn out, and I wrote about it. I wrote about everything, but in the diary I romanticized it something awful and I knew at the time I was doing it, I mean, I knew I was exaggerating and so forth, but I wrote it that way because I wanted it to be that way. Look," she said, "I was fourteen."

"Right."

"Oh well, anyway, one night Daddy found the diary in my desk drawer. I think he must have pried it open and read something. You could pull it apart a little because the strap wasn't all that tight and you could read sideways into the pages. Anyway, the next thing I know I went in there and he was sitting on my bed, reading the thing with this awful, red-faced look.

"He put the book down and motioned for me to come in and told me to close the door and I was scared. I can't tell you how scared I was. I don't know if I was ever that scared again, except when I had the abortion. . . ."

"The abortion?"

"Well, I'll tell you about it in time. So, I was in the room with him and I was scared, really scared, and he made me sit across from him and he kept on reading. And it was awful. Really awful, because as I sat there and he read, his hands were shaking, and he lit a cigarette and they were shaking even worse trying to do that, and I had to sit there and watch him read and every time I tried to say anything he would look up at me with this ugly face he'd never used on me before, would point his finger at me and tell me to shut up, and then, of course, I would, and he just kept on reading.

"I tried to read upside down where he was in the book and I could see he was already to the parts with Richard and me and, as I read upside down I could see he was getting to a part, I mean, he was already way past the part where I talked about going all the way with him, but I could see he was getting to a part that was really romantic, really phony and made-up and I just couldn't stand for him to know that much about me and I grabbed the book and ran out of the room and he chased me and almost had me except that Mother came walking through the hall just then and as I passed her and she saw him chasing me she grabbed his arm, in a reflex I think it must have been, like, hold on here, what's this about, and I got to the bathroom and locked the door and tore out the pages and flushed them away.

"And then when I came out Daddy must have been talking to her because they took me by the arms, one on each side of me, and led me into the living room and started in on me. Is this true? Is this true? They just kept on. 'Did you' . . . what is it they were saying, oh yeah, 'Did you fornicate with this boy?' That's what they kept asking me, fornicate, like it was something awful, I'd never thought of it that way, but I did the strangest thing then, I just told them no, that it was all a lie and that I had been making it up in the diary just to pretend. And of course they didn't believe me and kept at me, giving me the third degree and it just went on all night and I kept denying it and Mother sided with me for a while and Daddy got madder and madder, said he knew I was lying and you have to remember back then how big a deal being a virgin was, I mean, it was like the ultimate sin to lose your virginity, and Daddy was getting madder and madder and, you know, thinking about it now I don't think there is anything I could have done that would have gotten them that upset. Not anything at all. Not stealing, not flunking a course, not anything. Isn't that weird? But, so it went on and I was crying the whole time and just absolutely worn out and they were just like, by the end, somehow Mother was on his side, furious that I'd done it, and I was crying and still lying, and the harder they pushed me the more I lied, the more furious they got and after a few hours I was so tired I was about to fall over right there on the couch and they were still going strong and then Mother said that they were going to take me to the doctor the next day and have him examine me to see if I was still a virgin and that all my lies would be exposed then.''

Sally walked into the kitchen and drank the rest of her ice tea and reached for his. ''May I?'' she asked and he nodded yes.

''So they were in this fury, this compulsion to prove me wrong and Daddy said that we didn't have to go to a doctor to prove it, that he and Mother could examine me right then and find out and I just went nuts, let me tell you, I really did, and I started crying and running around the room, and they took hold of me and forced me to sit back down and said they'd give me one more chance, you know, that old thing, but I was so far gone with the lies I couldn't stop, so they took me, and I mean took, like dragged me, into the bedroom and shut the door and Mother told me to take off my panties and I wouldn't do it and they both grabbed me, they hurt my arms they held me so tight, I remember they hurt for days afterwards, and they pulled me down on the bed and pulled up my skirt,'' she said and looked at him, but though he knew she was looking at him he wouldn't look back and just shook his head.

''You want me to go on?''

He shrugged.

''I don't have to,'' she said.

''Go ahead.''

"All right. But let me say something. It's really strange telling this. I have never said a word to anyone about this, and yet in telling it, it's like I'm telling it about someone else. Like it happened to someone else."

"I wish," he said.

"So I was still fighting and Daddy had my wrists and Mother was down at my legs and I was turning and screaming, God knows I wonder what the neighbors thought, and then Daddy squeezed my wrists so hard and twisted them around to make me be still and I just went limp. I just gave up. I just went dead. I just wanted it over with. And Mother examined me and Daddy held me and I just lay there with my eyes closed and then, the strangest thing, after she claimed to have found out the truth, that I was no longer a virgin, everything let go, I mean, literally, he let go of me and the anger and madness let go, and after I admitted it was true, they seemed relieved. And happy. I swear they were. Everything changed, and Mother, who had been so vicious, as vicious as Daddy when I never thought she could be, held me while I cried and then ran a hot bath for me and took me in there and the night I never thought would end finally ended and I fell into the deadest sleep you could ever imagine.

"Except later," she said, and looked up as if she were trying to see it more clearly, "either Daddy came back in or I dreamed it but it was like I couldn't breathe all of a sudden and I couldn't wake up and I halfway did and there was his mad face and then it was like one of those dreams where you can't get loose from something and you can't wake up and just at the point where you think you might actually never come back you do, like just short of real death, that was what it was like, and then, at six-thirty, when the alarm went off, I got up, got dressed, went to school and just kept on going. As if nothing had happened. Can you imagine that? Really. But I did it and no one ever knew a thing.

"And that's what's so crazy. Neither that nor anything else, like what I'm going to tell you next if you want to still go on, was ever talked about again. I mean, it happened, but it didn't happen. Like the shame of it all was just too much. For everyone. Know what I mean?''

''I guess so.''

''Are you still with me?''

''Yeah.''

''Can I come and sit beside you now?''

''No.''

''Please.''

''Not just yet.''

''Then maybe I better not go on.''

''I think you better.''

''But you're pulling away from me. More. I can feel it.''

''I'm not. I'm still here. I'm just waiting for whatever it is coming next.''

''I don't know,'' she said.

''Do you want to tell me?''

''I do. I really do. I just want to be sure it's right.''

''Then go on.''

''Okay,'' she said. ''I will. Because it's making me feel better.''

''Good.''

''So, after that, everything changed. Between me and my parents, I mean. I don't know, Daddy got weird, wouldn't talk to me, wouldn't look at me, acted like a jealous lover if you want to know the truth, like I'd betrayed him. He used to follow me on my dates. I mean, I knew it, and we'd see him, he would have found out from Mother where we were going and of course we never went where we said, but he'd show up sometimes, in the car, and we'd lose him, it would turn into a game, he'd chase us and we'd lose him and those poor little boys I'd be out with wouldn't know what to think, they just didn't know what they'd gotten into, but you know what?'' she asked and was quiet for a moment as she thought about it. ''You know what? If he hadn't been so crazy about it and so perverse about it, I wonder if I wouldn't have eased up a little. I just wonder.''

''I don't know.''

''They were both so puritanical and so all twisted up, about everything, really, they just drove me to it and what else could I do? I didn't have anyone. I didn't have anyone who wanted me or loved me.''

''Seems like you found plenty of guys for that,'' he said.

''No. Not from them.''

''Whose baby was it?''

''I don't know. I was so out of control I don't even know. But I got pregnant, I missed two periods and that made me, let me think, I guess that made me about ten weeks at the time I finally told my father.''

''Why didn't you tell your mother? Why tell him?''

''I don't know. We were out in the car, I guess he was picking me up from somewhere, and I told him. It just happened. I couldn't keep quiet about it anymore, and he didn't say anything at first, but a little bit later, I swear I think he gloated, like, 'I told you so,' or, like, well, 'I knew it,' and he just did all the wrong things after that. He called me a bitch and a slut and was mad as hell and all I wanted was understanding and help and he wouldn't let me tell Mother. He said it'd kill her and then I told him I wanted to have the baby, because by then, I had decided that. When I first thought I was pregnant, I immediately thought of an abortion, but you couldn't get them back then, I mean people had heard of them, had heard of people getting them but no one I knew really knew where to go or how to get one, but the more I thought about it the more I thought I'd just go ahead and have the baby and give it away to someone who wanted one, but then after I told him about it, he said no way. He said we'd all be ruined if anyone found out and that he'd have to see about getting it fixed. That's the way he said it, 'Getting it fixed.' And so a week later he took me down into colored town and had it done.''

"Just like that?"

"Just like that. All I remember is being so scared I thought I was going to die, that I would never come out of that little house alive, and that I prayed that I would be forgiven and that I would live. But here I am."

"Yeah."

"And now I can't get pregnant. It's a punishment on me, but damnit, it shouldn't be on me. I was innocent. In a way I really was. I was crazy and I was wild but I was innocent at the same time. I didn't know what to do. I couldn't do anything, really. I could only do what people told me to do. That's all I knew to do. Only what people told me to do."

"Someone should have killed him long ago," he said.

"We can't think that. It's just that I wish, I really do, I could have come to you in better shape. If I could just make up for it. If I just could."

"It's a little late."

"But it isn't. That's why I've gone ahead and told all of this. Don't you see? I'm going to be better now. You can never tell what might happen. You know how things change. I've read in magazines about people who couldn't get pregnant and then they adopt a baby and then something happens and then they do. It's because they've let go of something and then it happens. Don't you see?"

"I don't know what I see. I see, on the one hand, that I ought to be magnanimous, but if you want to know the truth, I feel like shit. And I hate your father worse than ever now."

"But it won't do any good to hate him. You can't. I've tried. It doesn't work. It doesn't affect him. It doesn't change a thing. It just wears you out. He's still there and it's still there and he's always going to be there. You just have to let it go. Just like I just did. I feel so much better. The only thing I'm worried about is you."

"Thanks a lot."

"Come back to me, honey," she said and the phone rang and it was her father, who said, "I'm coming up."

He was calling from a pay phone.

"I have nowhere else to go. I can't go home. I can't find Angie. I've got to talk with you."

"Don't," Robert heard her say and knew it was him. "You must not do that. Not now. Not tonight. It's impossible."

"I am coming," he told her. "I have nowhere else to go."

"He's coming here? Now?" Robert asked when she hung up.

"Yes."

"But why?"

"He didn't say. He just said he couldn't go home."

"What's wrong at home?"

"I don't know. I think I'll call Mother and have her stop him."

"Can she do that?"

"If she wants, she can."

She called, but no one answered.

"I don't want to see him," Robert said.

"Neither do I."

"As a matter of fact, I don't think I will."

"What do you mean?"

"I think I'll leave."

"Don't do that."

"No. I think I will."

"But I need you now. I thought if I told you all about that . . ."

"I wish I had never picked up that journal. How things change once you know about something, when before, oh well," he said, "I just can't believe it. I feel absolutely trashed. Thirty-seven men. Which makes me number thirty-eight and what does that make me?"

"Just stop it. Please."

"Abortions and examinations on the bed and God only knows what else there is to find out and now he's coming up and if I stay around here I just might kill him. I really might. I don't know you anymore. I don't know who I am, either."

"But baby," she said, "I'm the same. I really am."

"You're not. And I can't face him tonight. Much less for the rest of my life. It seems like you two should have worked all this out before I came along. It seems like," he said, getting up and walking out, "you should have worked out a lot of things a long time before you met me. I'll leave you two alone to do it tonight."

"But if you leave now . . . I mean, please, what do you want me to do? He's still my father."

"Do whatever you want. Just leave me out of it."

At eight o'clock Margaret knew Ervin had really left her there for the entire night. She turned on the exhaust fan to air out the stuffy room. When she turned it on, she remembered that it vented out the roof into a sloped metal cage on top of the shingles above the bathroom. She yelled into the fan. She put one foot on the edge of the tub and the other on the toilet and called for help. She tried to call in a dignified manner. She said, "Please someone. I'm locked in. Can anyone hear me?" Then she turned the fan off and tried it that way.

All I can do is wait, she thought. And hope.

She took the towels from the linen closet and made a mattress on the floor. She folded a pillow from them and lay down. The cold-water faucet dripped in the sink. She had not known it dripped. Ervin must not know it dripped because he would have fixed it. Any sound kept him awake. No. Not anymore. He took so many pills and drank so much NyQuil it was a wonder he woke up each morning.

The furnace ignited and warm air blew from the grill in the wall. It blew for ten minutes and then stopped. A half hour later, it blew again. She took off her shoes and put her bare feet directly on the grill. She leaned against the side of the tub. There was nothing to do with her anger but forget it. She was furious but had no way to show it.

She was hungry. She had not eaten supper and remembered the chicken and salad and wondered where Ervin was and imagined him in a nice restaurant, being pleasant with the waitress in a very low-key way, letting on nothing, a felon in flight, a murderer of possibilities, a thief of happiness, a man guilty of so much, yet never standing trial for anything.

On the road, in the middle of a tract of paper-company woodlands, the man in flight passed a solitary house. The house was back from the road a hundred feet and was dark except for one room where a single overhead bulb hung from a cord.

Ervin saw this as he sped by in the camper, his home on wheels, more elaborate and better-equipped than the old shack. He glanced briefly, but saw clearly into the house. An eerie white light shone from a television set. It glowed more brightly than the bare bulb. A man in a straight-backed chair leaned his elbows on a green wooden table.

It was remarkable how thoroughly this man in flight, guilty of so much domestic violence, captured this solitary vision of home, this still life of the house on the edge of thousands of acres of trees, lit by a single light, illuminating one person in a room nearly empty of furniture save the chair and the table and the unearthly glow of the television.

Sally stood beside the knee-high plastic end table on which the telephone sat and watched as Robert came across the room, intent on leaving, ignoring her, going out.

"This is wrong," she said.

He did not answer. She followed him across the room.

"I haven't done anything to you."

He went out the door. She followed him onto the porch. She was barefoot. The porch was wooden and sagged in the center where the rain, which splashed off the flat rock that served as a step, had rotted the flooring and the sill beneath. The floor was cold but not as cold as the air.

"Get rid of that old man," he said.

He went to his truck. The engine fired immediately, still warm from the drive home. He backed out of the parking spot and out of the range of the porch light. He drove off and did not look back.

He did not look back because he did not want to see his wife standing on the porch barefoot and weeping, with her hand on the dog's head, resting gently as it had on his arm.

He did not look back because he did not want to see her lips move or hear her say, ''Don't leave me,'' and he drove down the driveway, blinding himself by turning his head so that out of the corner of his eyes he would not see her raise her hand in a gesture for him to stop, or know that she was saying, once more, sobbing now from the betrayal of what childhood had promised to the possible end of her own charmed marriage, sobbing now with the distant woods and the open field and the black cold sky a vision of emptiness, and saying into the night, ''Don't leave me,'' and pausing, ''Please don't.''

She went inside. She locked the door. She took a blanket off the bed and wrapped herself in it and sat beside the dying fire of the woodstove, and she waited.

At eight-fifteen Angie got the message to call Ervin but there was no answer. At eight-thirty she left Darlene with Mrs. Scholtz and went to find out what was going on. She did not want to lose him. Disregarding the pension and the new condominium, he was the only man who had even been nice to her, been kind to her, talked with her, respected her, listened to her, and asked nothing in return.

She felt sorry for him and she felt sorry for Margaret and she was worried because there was no answer and she had to know where she stood, and so she drove to his house. She knew where he lived because she had driven by before to see what kind of place it was. His camper was not there, but the car was. She drove down the street and then back up, and from neither direction could she see any lights in the house.

She parked on the side of the road two houses down and walked right up. She rang the bell, certain no one was home and not wanting to look suspicious should anyone have been watching. She rang it again and then walked around back. She was afraid of what she might find.

She could see where she was going from the illumination of an area light on a utility pole in the backyard next door. She tried the door and then walked to the other side.

Margaret heard the bell ring twice. She called. She beat on the wall and called and yelled and Angie heard her and stopped.

"Hello?" Angie called, but not loudly enough.

She listened to Margaret beating on the wall and calling for help and then she picked up a rock and beat on the brick wall opposite the noise. Margaret beat back from the inside and called louder this time and Angie followed her directions to the spare key and came in the side door.

She turned on the lights as she went from room to room, and as she did, she noticed the furniture, the decor, the cleanliness of the house, the pictures on the wall, all the domestic evidence of the other woman in Ervin's life, and, lighting her way across the house, and following the sound of Margaret's voice, ended up in his room.

The moment she entered the room she knew his smell and she saw his bed and she knew from what he had told her he slept alone and she looked at the unadorned walls and she heard Margaret through the door directly in front of her and she feared coming face-to-face with this woman for whom she felt so sorry and whose marriage she was about to destroy.

"I'm here. Are you there?"

"I'm here," Angie called. "How do I get you out?"

"The lock is on the outside. My husband, oh, never mind, it's right there, in the knob. Do you see it?"

Angie opened the door. She looked at Margaret. She

looked right in her eyes and though she tried not to look down at the leg, she did, and saw two perfectly formed legs.

"How did you hear me?" Margaret asked. "Who are you? I thought you were one of my neighbors."

"Oh," she said, scrambling to compute the good leg and figure out what next to do or say. "I, well, I was walking by, really I was looking for someone's house and I had come up to your door and after I rang the bell—did you hear the bell?— I heard you calling."

"Well, I'm glad of that. It was silly of me to lock myself in there. My husband's gone out of town and I don't know what I would have done without you."

Angie nodded.

"I'm Margaret Neal, by the way."

"I'm Sa—Sara Taylor," she said.

"Oh," Margaret said, and began to think.

"I guess I better go now. I'm glad you're safe."

"Why not stay a minute. Have some coffee."

"Well, I shouldn't really," she said.

"Oh come on. It's not every day you're a hero, is it?"

She sat at the kitchen table while Margaret made the coffee and looked at her in Ervin's chair with her legs crossed and looked at her legs, as well, drawn to them by the sight of those familiar blue-gray crepe-soled shoes postal employees who had to be on their feet all day often wore.

"You're not really Sara Taylor, are you?" she asked as she put her coffee down in front of her.

"Well of course I am. Whatever are you talking about?"

"You're Angela Taylor and you came here looking for Ervin."

"You're crazy," she said.

"You are Angela Taylor and you did come here looking for Ervin because the last time you saw him you were being chased down by me in that car," she said and pointed out the window, "sitting right there in the driveway. Right?"

Angie did not answer. Margaret studied her. She saw a

woman older than her years, a woman who looked to be in her late thirties, but probably wasn't. A woman who'd had a hard life, probably much harder than hers. A woman with an acne-scarred face, at least fifteen pounds overweight, and with fingernails bitten, uniformly, all the way down to the quick.

"I've got to smoke," Angie said. "I'm trying to quit," she said, still lighting it.

"I'm right, aren't I?"

"Maybe."

"And you came here looking for Ervin? Is that what you did? You came here looking for my husband," she said, staking the claim with the word *my*.

"Maybe I did."

"And what were you going to do if you found him?"

"Maybe I didn't care whether I did or not. Maybe I was just looking to see . . ." she took a big drag, ". . . what kind of woman would follow her husband and try to break his door down and chase him across town in a car. About what kind of woman that was."

"Me," Margaret said.

"Yes. I see. You."

"Yes, and I see something too. I see a woman who doesn't have the foggiest idea what she's getting into. I see a woman who's about to make the biggest mistake of her life."

"I doubt that."

"I don't. I know it. I'm married to him, don't forget. I see someone with her hands shaking who just better, for everyone's good, pack it up and forget about all of us."

"Ervin might have something to say about that."

"He won't have anything to say about it. Let me tell you something, girl," Margaret said, "you can't take him away from me. You can't because he doesn't want to leave. If he did, he would have left me years ago. You understand what I'm saying?"

"You're wrong," she said. "You're wrong or I wouldn't be here."

"Oh is that right?"

"That's right. If I didn't know he wanted me more than you, I wouldn't have come looking for him to save him from some crazy woman like you."

"GET OUT OF HERE!" Margaret screamed at her and Angie started out.

"THERE'S NOTHING LEFT BETWEEN YOU TWO," Angie screamed back at her and she ran out the door. "He loves me," she said.

Margaret chased her into the yard and spun her around by her arm.

"He doesn't love you. He can't. I'm the closest thing he ever got to love and it scared the hell out of him. If he left me for you, he'd make your life such hell you wouldn't know what hit you."

"That's your opinion," she said and pulled her arm loose.

"Stop," Margaret said. "I'm sorry I yelled at you. Don't leave yet. We really ought to talk about this."

"What's there to say?"

"You need to understand what's going on. What you're doing. Have you been married before?"

"Yes."

"Well," Margaret said and then realized they were standing in the cold rain. "Hey, why are we standing out here in this rain? Come on back in."

"I don't think so," Angie said.

"All right, then. Be that way. This is what I want to tell you. You don't know him. You can't imagine what you're getting yourself into. I know you think he's in love with you but he can't be because he can't love anyone. He's not able to. He just isn't."

"But you love him."

"I do. I love him for what he was, and what he might be again. Do you understand me?"

"I've got to go," she said.

"I'm trying to be nice to you, you stupid girl," Margaret said. "But if you want to be that way, I can, too. Don't ever come back here. Don't ever see him again."

"I'll wait and hear that from him," she said.

"Leave town," Margaret said to her back, following her. "Stay away from him and from me. Get another job. Do it for your own good. You can't have him. You won't get him. He's mine."

And Angie, having met the immovable force face to face, having met the octopus of possessive madness and tangled with it, drove home, astonished at the tough woman she had found when she thought she was going to just blow her away, astonished at the good leg and seeing a glimpse of the trouble she was getting into. She began to fear the entanglement of the desperate situation, fearing for herself and her daughter, fearing, having just been through it herself last year, the nightmarish reality of the eviscerated marriage, the dark presence of the deadly broken taboos and the lonely empty nights of the broken life.

She drove back, then, homesick for her daughter, for the steady trusting love that she shared with her. She drove home empty and shaking inside like waking from a bad dream where the revelation of what she'd seen cut too deeply to go any further and jerking awake was the only way out, and then, in the waking, the truth that had been made visible in the dream, the truth of the destructive madness of the unmended, selfish heart, the truth stayed with her as she drove home to her daughter, and as she held her and felt, at least there, a steady, perfect balance of love.

Sally waited alone. She waited in that desperate, paralyzed way the child waits to be spanked, having been told to do so. She waited in the same way the patient stands immobile for the needle, the way the victim waits before the hollow barrel of the gun, waiting to be shot.

She curled up under the blanket and fell asleep for a moment. The fire was out when she jerked back awake and she pulled up the afghan her mother had made and given her when she went off to college, and wrapped that around her, as well.

The dog scratched on the door and the cat jumped up on a table on the porch and looked in at her through the window. The dog scratched again and sounded a faint and pitiful whine along with it and the cat put one paw on the cold windowpane and stared at Sally until Sally acknowledged his exotic countenance.

"I can't get up now," she said. "Just wait."

The dog scratched again and she thought how many coats of yellow ochre she had put on that door trying to make up for years of dog scratching and she arose looking like a rag lady or a refugee from the faded films of World War II.

"It's not much warmer inside," she told the animals, but it wasn't true. There were those soft chairs and the pillows and no cold wind and the animals knew where they wanted to be, with her, in the house, a place, she thought, she ought to leave.

If I'm not here, then what?

She opened the oven door and turned the dial to 450 and lit all the burners as well, and she pushed the kitchen chairs near the stove and sat on one and put her feet on the other and she thought about leaving until she realized that it was possible, quite possible, and, indeed likely, that Robert would return to be with her and how horrible it would be for him to meet that old man alone, and so she waited in the kitchen and listened for the sound of someone coming down the drive, and she even prayed a little, casually and without effort, making a few deals while she was at it, for things to come out right.

At nine Robert parked his truck in downtown Chapel Hill. He had failed to take a jacket. The heater in the old truck just barely worked, and the cold air from where the battery had rotted out the metal under the floor on the driver's side blew into the cab.

He sat in the truck and chewed on his knuckles and thought about a scene from his wife's journal, where she had written about a time on the beach on the Outer Banks where she walked alone during one vacation when she was a freshman in college, and saw, in the distance, someone come down the empty and isolated beach and how she met him and how she thought that one could not not speak, one could not not talk and make contact, she had written, how one could not, in the middle of miles of empty sand and beach, meet another decent human being and not make contact and recognize his existence, a metaphor come to life, how one could not leave without giving something to the other person, so that in the leaving, she had written, each takes with him or her something that makes life a little easier, a little better, if only for a little while.

And how it had hurt when he'd read that, because how true it was and how truly touching it was and how truly like the generous soul of his precious wife to see it and do something about it.

He got out and looked in the window of a restaurant where a wide-screen television lit up one end of the room and a basketball game was on. Further down the street a girl stood in front of a clothing store. She wore knee-high boots and a mini-skirt and stockings and a vinyl jacket with a furry collar. She looked sideways as he slowed down to see her better.

That girl's a whore, he thought. She's waiting for someone.

He stopped at the next window. The girl remained where she was. He looked at her face. She was young. She might have been sixteen or as old as nineteen. It was hard to tell.

People passed behind them. The sidewalk was brightly lit. He looked back at her and saw her face was red and puffy.

Drug addict, he thought. Or drunk.

"Excuse me," he said. She looked up. Hard as she tried to hide it, he saw that she had been crying.

"I'm sorry," he said. "Are you all right?"

She nodded and then looked down.

"Can I help in any way?"

"I'm okay. Thanks, though."

Damn, he thought. The night of the weeping women. "You know, it's strange. I'm having a kind of bad night myself."

She nodded.

"Well, if you're really okay," he said, and started to leave.

"You don't have to go."

"All right. You want to get out of this rain and go somewhere?" he asked.

"Where?" she asked. "Where do you go to cry?"

"Good point," he said. "Where does a person go to cry? Well, let's see. I live too far away to go to my place, and it wouldn't work, anyway."

She noticed his wedding band.

"I guess not," she said.

"Restaurants and bars wouldn't be right, would they?"

"Not unless they served Kleenex."

"That's pretty good," he said and they both smiled.

"I just need to talk, really. That's what usually makes me feel better."

"We could sit in my truck. That's all I can think of."

They walked to the truck and stayed an awkwardly long distance apart, as if in fear of touching each other.

"Here it is," he said. "Not much, but it's home."

"You're kidding."

"I'm kidding."

The cab was high and rounded something like a dome. The seat was long and wide and high so that their legs hung straight down as if sitting in real chairs.

"This is a nice old truck," she said. "It is old, isn't it?"

"Yeah. About twenty years old."

"That's older than me."

"I thought it was."

"How old are you?" she asked.

"Thirty. Or so."

"So's my boyfriend."

"Oh."

"He threw me out."

"Literally?"

"What?"

"Did he actually throw you, like toss you out?"

"Oh sure. That's nothing new."

"Did he hurt you?"

"Not much."

"You can tell me about it if you want."

"It's nothing. Just one of those things I get myself into."

"What're you going to do?"

"I don't know. That's the problem. I don't have anywhere to go. I don't even have any money. He pushed me out the door and threw me my coat and my purse but I don't have, but, let's see, about eight dollars," she said, and emptied her wallet into her lap. "That's about it."

"Well," he said. "I've got a little and if you're feeling like it we could go to a restaurant. I'm starved. I kind of ran out without supper, myself."

"I don't know. I'm scared I might run into him."

"Oh."

"Let's just drive around. Back when I had my own car I used to drive around by myself, you know, when I got down, had a bad day, you know. Just ride around going nowhere, doing nothing."

"Sounds good," he said.

"You're nice."

"Thanks."

"You're a real nice guy," she said and patted him on his shoulder in a strangely unfeminine gesture, the way a man might pat his son on the shoulder and tell him, "Good job, son."

He turned the blower to high and pushed the heater control all the way over. The fumes coming through the holes in the floor were bad and both of them had their windows down.

"I used to work there," she said, and pointed to a chicken-and-biscuit take-out restaurant.

"Did you?"

"Yes. After I quit the mill. I should have never quit. Long story, though. Lots of long stories in my life," she said.

"I think I'm just going to have to get something to eat."

"Okay. But listen, mister," she said, and then, as if just realizing it, said, "I don't even know your name."

"Robert."

"Mine's Catherine. With a C."

"Nice name."

"Listen, Robert. Don't get me wrong, or anything, but how much money do you have on you?"

"Not much."

"I was asking because here we are both riding around in the cold with nowhere to go and why, I was thinking, don't we just go to a motel, get a nice warm room and get comfortable. If you have enough money, I'd love to get off the streets."

Angie hugged Darlene so hard and so long the little girl wondered about it.

"Ouch, Mommy. That's too hard."

"I needed it. It felt good to Mommy."

"Where did you go? Why did Mrs. Scholtz have to come over?"

"I had to go somewhere," she said. "I thought I did, anyway. But Mommy's back now. She made a mistake. Someone told her a lie."

"Who?"

"Just someone."

"What mistake?" Darlene asked.

"She almost got in trouble."

"What kind of trouble?"

"She almost got into something bad, just like something bad that happened to her a little while ago."

"But what?"

"It's nothing. Not anymore. I'm home and I'm going to be very careful now and you and Mommy are going to do lots of things together and we're going to have a great life."

"Here in this old ratty apartment?" Darlene asked.

"Maybe we better move," she said. "To a not-so-ratty old apartment. How about that?"

"To a nice big house? With an indoor swimming pool?"

"Maybe," Angie said. "Maybe we can do that someday. Right now, though, it's bedtime. Come on. I'll tell you a story."

"Which one?" she said and climbed back in where she'd been when she heard her mother come in and send Mrs. Scholtz away.

"Your favorite."

"Okay. But let me tell it to you. I'll be the Mommy."

"All right. You be the Mommy."

"If you were a bird, and you flew away, I'd be a tree and you'd have to come back to me."

"That's right," Angie said.

"If you were a fish and you swam away, I'd be a fisherman and bring you back with a net."

"That's right, honey. Keep on."

"And if you were a bad bunny and you ran away, I'd make myself as big as the world and I'd always be with you everywhere you went."

And Angie curled up beside Darlene and together they went to sleep, balancing along that fragile line of parent and child.

The telephone rang and Sally answered it and it was not Robert and it was not her father. It was, of course, her mother.

"I knew he'd call you. I knew he'd go running to you. I just knew it," her mother said.

"Well, I don't know what to do about it. Where were you, anyway?"

"Locked in his bathroom."

"What?"

"I'll tell you about it when I get there," she said.

"Get where? Here. Not you too, Mother. I can't take it," she said and then thought about it. "But yes, maybe that's best. Maybe you better come on. Now. Hurry. Maybe that's the best thing that could happen," she said. "But how will you get here?"

"I've got my license now and I've got the car and nothing's going to stop me. And when I get there," she said, "I'll have him right where I want him."

"Can you drive this far alone? In the dark?"

"Of course I can. I've got maps. Why can't I do anything anybody else can do? You just hold him," she said, "until I get there."

"I don't think I'll do that," Sally said.

"Or get Robert to. I think I see the light at the end of the tunnel," she said. "I met his girlfriend."

"Oh no."

"It was good. I've got so much to tell you. It made me see things so much more clearly. Anyway," she said, "I'm coming now. I'll be there before you know it."

Robert gave Catherine some money and sent her to wait in line for a box of chicken while he went to a pay phone to call his parents to see if he could come home for a few days and get things sorted out. He also wanted to tell them they had been right.

When he heard his mother's voice, he thought for the first time that night he might cry. The sound of her voice took him far back and he wanted to say, he could hear himself saying as he saw himself running and being held and comforted while he wept, "Mother, Mother darling, I'm coming back, I'm coming home, please hold me, please take me in and tell me all is forgiven." He could feel that in the tightness of his throat as he told them, "In a way, I just wanted to say that maybe I've done some wrong things and made some wrong decisions and maybe, after all, you were right. Not entirely, but maybe I made a mistake and maybe I should have known from that first time when I visited her family and something told me things were just not right but I just kept on, I mean, it's so hard to see what people don't want you to see. And that's why I've called because I thought that maybe, if it'd be all right, I could come down. I don't know, for a few days and, I don't know, just get things sorted out."

"Of course you can," his mother said.

"Of course you can," his father said.

"But what's happened?" his mother asked. "Tell us what brought this about."

"I can't. Not now."

"Is it an affair?"

"No."

"Then what could it be?"

"Just a lot of things," he said.

"Well, I was afraid this might happen," his mother said.

"It couldn't have worked out," his father said.

"Not ultimately," his mother said.

"Well," Robert started to say.

"I don't mean she isn't just as nice and sweet as can be," his mother said.

"We don't mean that," his father said.

"It's just that you come from two different worlds," she said.

"Anyway, it's over," his father said, still on the extension.

"And we're here for you," she said.

"I didn't say it was over," Robert said.

"Well, whatever it is, we're here and we're ready to help

and you come on home for a few days and tell us all about it.''

"And if it is time for a divorce, we'll help you with a lawyer.''

"We'll get you a good one," his mother said. "Half of everything is yours," she added.

"Even if she did pay for most of it," his father said.

"Don't let her get the farm," she said. "Even though we've never even seen it, real estate is always worth holding on to.''

"You just work out a settlement with her," his father said.

"We'll talk about it," his mother said. "And if it really is over, then we can just thank God it's not been any worse than it has.''

"You've learned something, anyway," his father said.

"He has," his mother said back to him.

"I knew he would pull out of it someday," he told her.

"I know you said that," she said back to him, and while they discussed him with each other he just kind of faded away on the other end of the phone as the sound of their voices brought him back from that scene of being held and comforted to what really was in store for him when he went back, days and days and maybe for the rest of his life of telling him what to do and with whom to do it, and it wasn't too hard to go from there to just why he had fallen so in love with Sally and just what there was without her, just what there was where he had come from and while they talked to each other, completely forgetting he was there, he quietly and ever so lightly hung up the phone and walked back to Catherine, thinking, for a moment, until he saw her bright and expectant face, that he might just go on back to the farm.

"Ready?" she asked.

"Well," he said.

"Oh, come on," she said. "We'll have a good time.''

"Okay," he said. "Just for a little while.''

The motel had a double bed and a table instead of a desk

and a wooden chair at that table and on either side of the table were two other chairs. One was a contemporary design, with black plastic cushions and varnished wood arms. The other was wrought iron with a canvas seat and was circular and looked like something that had once been on a patio or near a pool.

The carpet was brown and spotted. The room was cold and the air conditioner was also the heater. Robert turned the dial to heat and the fan to high and Catherine set the box of chicken and two cans of Pepsi on the table.

"It's not that bad, is it?" she asked.

"No. Not bad at all."

"No television, though. You have to ask for it."

"Never heard of that."

"They're afraid people will steal them. You can get one, if you want. It's just a dollar extra. They make you sign for it, though. Show identification, you know."

"Do you want one?" he asked.

"Do you?"

"I don't know. What's on?"

"What's today?"

"Tuesday. I think it is, anyway."

"Yes. It is. I remember now."

"I don't want to watch anything."

"I don't blame you. What do you do, by the way?" she asked.

"I'm a carpenter."

"My boyfriend hangs sheetrock. You don't seem like a carpenter to me. Not like the ones I've known."

"I am, but only temporarily, you might say. Passing through on my way somewhere else."

"That's neat. I like that. My boyfriend and this other guy he works with make a hundred dollars a day, sometimes. Each."

"That's more than I make."

"Sometimes they don't though. Am I talking too much?"

she asked as he checked on the air conditioner–heater. "Or too fast?"

"Not to me."

"Sometimes I do. That thing'll heat up in a little while. It takes in the cold air here," she said and went over and pointed to the grills along the bottom, "and converts it to hot air and blows it out here, but it has to change the air in the room a couple of times before it can really start doing any good."

"How'd you know that?"

"My daddy was a furnace repairman. I used to go on the jobs with him when I was little. Before he left us."

"Oh."

"Let's eat," she said. "I'm suddenly hungry myself."

"Okay. White or dark?"

"White, if you don't mind."

"I don't."

She handed him a napkin and opened the drinks and he took the chicken from the box and gave her a piece. She put the pop-tops from the cans on her little fingers.

"I used to wear these when I was little, you know, pretending I was married, and all."

"Yes."

"I used to want to be married. Real bad. I dreamed about it all the time. Now I don't."

"I know what you mean."

"I used to watch my parents fight. My old man used to hit my mother, oh hell, he used to hit her so hard I couldn't believe she could take it. She never went down, though. I never saw her fall or flinch."

"Sounds awful."

"She'd hit him back later. When he wasn't expecting it. They fought all the time. I used to want to be married to show them I wouldn't be like them."

"That's common."

"Common?"

"People want to be different from their parents."

"Anyway, my boyfriend is just like my old man was. I can't believe I did that, you know, fell for someone just like him. When he gets drunk he slaps me around. He doesn't mean it, though. I don't think he does. Except,'' she said, contemplating further, "he slaps me around when he's sober, too.''

"What do you do?''

"Leave. Usually. Well, sometimes. Sometimes I don't mind. I guess sometimes I deserve it.''

The chicken was greasy. Robert used up his napkin. Catherine handed him another.

"I got to take these boots off. They're too tight. I knew they were too tight when I bought them, but it was the only size they had. I liked them, so I bought them anyway.''

She pulled at one while holding the chicken with her other hand.

"Stuck?''

"Yeah. Can you help?'' she asked.

He pulled them off. She wore pantyhose. The reinforced foot parts were torn.

"Thanks. Anyway,'' she said, "sometimes I deserve it, I guess, when I make him mad.''

She was small. With her high-heeled boots off, she was no more than five-one, he thought.

"Is he big?''

"Real big. Bigger than you. Bigger than my old man. And mean.''

"I gather.''

"Mean to other people. He'd beat the hell out of another guy as soon as look at him. One time I was talking to this guy I used to know, in the parking lot, we were just standing there talking and L.C., which is his name, my boyfriend, I mean, came out of the parts store—he was rebuilding a motor for a friend of his—and he saw me talking with this guy and he just walked up and slapped him with this long box gaskets come in.''

"No kidding?"

"He did."

She took off her jacket.

"I'm getting crumbs all over my good jacket," she said. She had on a blouse with two missing buttons.

"That's where he grabbed me when I ran," she said, noticing where he looked. "You can't really see my bra, can you?" she asked and looked down at herself sideways, trying to view her blouse as someone else would see it.

"I can't."

"I deserved it this time, I guess."

She sat in the round canvas chair. She turned sideways. Her skirt slid up as she slid down to get comfortable.

"You don't mind me sitting like this, do you?"

"Not at all. Make yourself at home."

"L.C. says I have a good body, but he doesn't want me showing it off. He gets mad when I wear tight clothes. Or short skirts."

"Is that what happened tonight?"

"How'd you know?"

"You're wearing a short skirt."

"Oh yeah. He came home and I was wearing this skirt, I like it best, and he asked me where I'd been all day and I wouldn't tell him and then he grabbed me and tried to fuck me—oops, I'm sorry."

"That's okay. I'm over twenty-one."

"I'm not, but, anyway, he was trying to fuck me, right there on the floor, and he had that goddamn sheetrock dust all over him and he smelled bad and I wouldn't let him."

"I don't blame you."

"I mean, I wouldn't have minded if he'd took a bath first."

"Right."

"But I hate that dust. You didn't mind when I said 'fuck,' did you?"

"No. Why should I?"

"Some people don't like cussing, but I do. I love it. I cuss all the time. Even when I'm alone I go around cussing at things.''

"It's a good way to get your frustrations out.''

"I just like the sound of the words.''

The room warmed up. The blower on the heater rattled as if something had come loose.

"You're nice to talk to,'' she said. "L.C. says I talk too much and too fast. Maybe I do. I like to talk. I like to talk about anything and everything. I'm interested in things, you know. I made good grades in school. I really did. I would have graduated if I hadn't run away.''

"You ran away?''

"Yeah. Last year. When I was sixteen. I was thinking of going back. To that school in Durham.''

"Which one?''

"Rutledge. I went over there once and talked with them. They were real nice. They wanted me to have my high school diploma first. I ought to go back one day. I'd be in the tenth grade, though. All my old friends would be graduating and I'd be in the tenth grade with all those creeps. That'd be hell, wouldn't it? It sure is hot in here now. Mind if I take off my pantyhose?''

"Go ahead.''

"You can turn around if you want. I don't wear underpants. I mean, L.C. used to get mad at me about it, but he said it sure made fucking a lot easier. I guess he wanted it both ways.''

She stood up and reached under her skirt.

"That's the way I like it. Sometimes around the house I go around naked all day. You want another piece of chicken? It's good tonight. It's not as greasy as it usually is.''

"Not right now.''

"You're married. I see your ring. What's your wife like? I bet she's real pretty.''

"Well. She is. She's tall and has long hair and nice skin and she works as a commercial artist.''

"Wow. That sounds fabulous. Did she draw any commercials I might have seen?"

"I don't know. I don't keep up with it."

"Maybe I could do that. I got a B+ in art in the eighth grade." She got out of the chair and started across the room. "I'm glad the blower's making all that noise. I've got to go to the bathroom. I hate to hear someone in the john, don't you?"

The bathroom was in a corner of the room. It had a birch-veneer door. Some of the veneer was torn off. She stopped just before she went in.

"Listen," she said. "I like you. I really do. I'm feeling really good now. I was just wondering, do you want to fuck when I come back out?"

Ervin turned into Sally's driveway. She did not hear him until the dog barked. For a moment, as she watched the lights coming up the dark drive, she imagined it was Robert. The size and bulk of the camper and the slow pace of its approach, however, dispelled that hope.

She had been awake since her mother's phone call. She had changed into jeans and a blouse and a wool sweater and a pair of warm hiking boots. The wood stove was out. The old ornate farm equipment thermometer tacked on the living room wall read fifty-one degrees. It was warmer in the kitchen where the gas oven and four burners were still lit.

Ervin tooted the horn and parked and Sally stopped in the middle of the kitchen as she heard him on the porch and watched the door thud against the lock as he tried to open it.

"Hey," he called. "Anybody home?"

She opened the door.

"What's the matter?" he asked as she pulled away from his embrace.

"I told you not to come up here."

"I know you did, but I had to."

"Well, if you've come up here, you're going to pay for it."

"I don't understand," he said and looked around the room after seeing the glow from the burners. "What's this?" he asked. "And where's Robert?"

"Never mind. Just come in here," she said. "Sit down there," she said and pointed him into a chair.

"Where's Robert?" he asked again.

"He's gone out for a little while. He heard you were coming and left."

"But why?"

"Because he's sick of you. Just like I am."

"I can't believe you just said that."

"I said it."

"But why?"

"You don't know, do you?"

"No I don't."

"I guess you don't," she said.

"I guess you're right," he said.

"Listen, Daddy. Don't push me tonight. I told you not to come up here and I'm real upset about it."

"I'm sorry."

"And about other things, too."

"But what have I done?"

"What you've done is not know what you've done. Ever."

"Listen," he said. "All I did was zip on up here to have a little talk with you. Granted it's a little late, but I had to."

"You're zipping-on-up days are over."

"You have never talked to me this way."

"I should have."

"What's happened? Who is this talking to me?" he asked the room in general.

"Listen to me," she said and slapped the table with her open hand. "You are not going to make me feel sorry for you with that look because you just can't anymore. You can't get to me anymore. You can't because I am through with this facade, this charade.''

"I didn't know we were playing charades," he said.

"STOP IT!" she screamed. "STOP YOUR GODDAMN JOKES AND LISTEN TO ME.''

He held up his arms as if to say, I surrender.

"It's time you started realizing what you're doing to the people around you and think about somebody besides yourself, and it's time you stopped treating Mother like dirt and it's time you stopped getting me mixed up in the middle of it all. You hear?''

He nodded.

"I mean, like, you don't even know what I'm talking about. I can tell by looking at you. I mean, it's like all that about painting the house and we kill ourselves to do it and you don't even say a word.''

He shrugged.

"It's like, all my goddamn life you have just run over me and Mother and anyone else you wanted to and then when things didn't work out like you wanted to, you have been, all my life, you hear, as long as I can remember, coming to me and putting me in the middle between you and Mother, always, since I was a child," she said. "Don't you know it?''

He shrugged again.

"IT'S TIME FOR IT TO STOP," she yelled. "It's time for you to get out of my life and off Robert's back and just disappear, how about it.''

"Listen," he said and stood up, pushing off the chair like an arthritic old man, destroyed and frightened to hear this from the one person he thought he could always count on, wiped out in spite of his offhand manner. "Listen," he said, "if I'd known things were going to be like this, I'd have never come. I sure would have never come," he said, and started out the door.

She stopped him.

"You're not going anywhere.''

"I'm going back to Wilmington. I'm going back to find Angie."

"No, you're not. You're going to stay here until Mother comes," she said and snatched the keys out of his hand.

"Your mother?" he asked. "But she can't be coming up here. It's not possible."

Margaret stopped in a little town. She looked at her map in the glow of the streetlight and saw she was in Dunn and was eighty miles from Sally's house. Maybe a little less. It was hard to tell from the map. It was nearly one A.M.

She drove on as if her life depended on it, as if her arrival would mark the end of a long fight, the cessation of hostilities, the end of the long battle of the sexes and she drove on as if she had, in the car, the evidence to convict and gain the confession of this man who had started it all, this guilty man, the end of the long delay in the trial, the judgment in her hands, mercy and compassion with her, as well. She drove to claim him, to claim the family honor, to forgive him, to allow him room to return, and, in doing so, fulfill the manifesto of her life, of the dream, of the marriage and the love and the family, of the parables of patience and duty and devotion, and of the triumph of good over evil.

Robert was still on the side of the bed with a half-eaten piece of chicken in his hand when Catherine came out of the bathroom, completely naked.

"Do you like my body? I do. My breasts are small, I know, but they're real firm. My nipples get big when I get excited. Sometimes they get big just when I get cold or something rubs against them. They're not all the way big yet. They're getting there, though."

She looked at herself in the mirror, and then resumed talking, but faster.

"I thought my breasts would get bigger when I got older but I guess they won't. I wonder if I'll be able to make enough milk to nurse a baby. I want to do that. I read about it in a magazine. It's good for the baby and for the mother, too."

She posed sideways and pulled her elbows back.

"My waist's small, though, and that makes them look bigger. What's your name, by the way? I forget if you told me. Oh yeah, Robert. I remember now. What was your last name?"

"Zilman."

"That's interesting. I never heard that before. It kind of sounds like a Jew name. Is that what it is? Or a Catholic one? Which is it?"

"Jewish, I guess."

"Really. That's great. I never knew a Jew before. Oh, wait a minute. I did. This girl in school was a Jew or her mother was, anyway, and she looked just like everyone else, you couldn't tell, not by looking at her anyway, but there was something different about her once you found out. People used to make fun of her but it never bothered me. I never minded niggers, either. Blacks, I mean. I try not to call them niggers anymore, like L.C. does. I call them blacks because they call themselves blacks, except I've heard them call each other nigger, too. A black boy fucked me one time. He was awfully light skinned, though. He was almost white, so I don't know if it really counts."

She put the leftover chicken in the box and took Robert's and wrapped it in a napkin and put it on top of the rest.

"I never had sex with a Jew before. This is going to be great. I love to do different things. That's one of the things that gets L.C. mad at me. I like to go places and meet people and do all kinds of things, and he just wants to stay home and drink. Or take dope. Do you drink? Oh yeah, you said you did, didn't you, or did I just make that up? I'm talking too fast again, aren't I? I'll try to slow down."

"You're doing just fine."

"I know I am. You're so nice. Do you want something to drink now? We could send out for something. A lot of men like to drink a little before they do it. I don't need to, though. Do you want anything? Good. L.C. says I come faster than any woman he was ever with. It's so nice and cozy in here now. I told you it would be. Aren't you going to take off your clothes?''

"Yes. I am," he said. "Let me go to the bathroom first."

"Sure. I did. I always go before I fuck. That way I don't have to get up when I'm finished and I can just lay there and feel it and just relax, you know, and it's so good, like it's one of the few times a person really feels relaxed, except when you do drugs, you know, some kinds anyway, but then when you come off them you feel worse, but I guess sometimes I feel bad after I've done sex, too."

When he came back she had put her knee-high boots back on but was otherwise still naked.

"You like this? I saw a woman posed in a magazine like this once, only she was on the bed, kind of like this," she said and lay on the bed and imitated the pose, "and it looked really neat. So sexy. I mean, if you think about it, why would boots make such a difference?"

"I don't know."

"I made love to a man once what kept his shoes and socks on. Talk about weird. He was real short and I guess he was trying to be as tall as he could, but talk about weird. I'm not kidding, I could feel his shoes and socks the whole time. Why don't you take your clothes off now?"

"I'm going to. I was just thinking for a second."

"I never think when I'm fucking. I just do it. If you start thinking about things it makes it harder to come, you know what I mean. You get messed up."

"I know."

"You do, don't you? You're the kind of guy what understands about women. I can tell. That's one of the things I like about you." She lay with her head toward the foot of the bed and put her feet on the wall over the headboard and looked at him upside down as he undressed.

"Oh look, you're not hard yet. L.C. always gets hard even before his clothes are off. Why aren't you hard yet? Don't you like me?"

"I do, but I was just . . ."

"Don't worry about it. I know what to do. Come on over here and get on the bed with me."

"Let me check the door first."

"Okay. What are you worried about? Nobody's coming in. Who even knows we're here?"

"Maybe L.C. followed you."

"The hell he did. If he had, he'd already be in here and would have killed you by now."

"Oh."

"You like the light on or off? I like it on so I can watch what's happening but we can turn it off if you want. That's good. Lie down beside me. I got a really great way to do it in mind. This man I met one time showed it to me. He was part Indian. His grandfather, he said, was a Lumbee Indian and anyway, this man showed me this kind of Indian way and I'll show it to you. You'll love it. Everybody I showed it to does."

"What do you want me to do?"

"Get like this," she said and then, for a second, for a long, long second, during which he saw L.C. coming through the door and during which he saw Sally weeping on the porch and during which he saw Ervin's ugly face and during which he saw, from a distance, himself, as well, for that long, visionary moment, he stopped.

"Mother is coming up here," Sally said.

"But," he said and looked closely at her, trying to determine how much she knew, "she doesn't even know where I went. She doesn't even know I'm here."

"Yes she does. She called and I told her you were coming."

"How could she call?"

"She used the telephone, like anyone else. Was there some reason you didn't think she could do that?" Sally asked.

"Well, not really."

"Of course there was. Don't lie to me," she said, "don't even begin to try to lie to me because I've got you this time and I know what you've been up to and this is the night, this is the moment when it's all going to stop and you're going to get your life in order and you're going to apologize to Mother and you and Mother are going to make up and you're going to forget this ridiculous thing with Angie and you're going to, finally, you HEAR ME," she began to scream again and then stopped, "get out of my life. Get out from between me and Robert and out of it for good."

"Give me the keys," he said.

"I will not."

"Give them to me or I will take them from you."

"You'll have to if you want them. But if you touch me, if you lay one hand on me, I'll kill you. I swear I will."

"Just give them to me. I'll leave. If that's what you want, I'll certainly do it."

"Nope."

"All right, listen," he said. "Let's sit back down. Let's have some coffee. Let's talk about it. But then, let me have my keys and get out of here."

"Are you afraid of Mother?"

"No. Don't be silly. I can see you're upset. It probably has something to do with Robert's leaving. If I've been the cause of it, then I'll have to own up to it and I'll quietly leave and let you two get on with things. If that's what you want."

"You're not going to get out of it that easy."

"Look. Just sit down. You're still my daughter and I love you very much." She made a face. "And I'm you're father and I always will be and that's that. You can't get rid of me, so let's talk about whatever you want. But first," he said, "let's make some coffee. Let me shut this stove off and while I make the coffee why don't you get your woodstove started."

"I'm standing right here. I'm not moving until Mother comes. You're not going out that door. Make your coffee if you want."

"Okay. I will. But one thing," he said, "let me call Angie. Just a quick call. I'll charge it to our phone. It won't cost you a thing."

"You're not going to call."

"I have to."

"You should have thought of that before you came up here."

She looked out the kitchen window and when she did, took a breath, like the first time she'd breathed since he walked in the door, and Ervin, hooked to his daughter by all those tangled threads of blood, felt her let go and came up behind her and put his hands on her shoulders.

"Baby," he said and she swung around so fast it knocked him back.

"Don't."

"ALL RIGHT, I WON'T," he screamed at her. "But you owe it to me to tell me what started all this. You really do."

She told him about the journal. She told him about the conversation with Robert and she started in again on the night of the examination.

"Don't you see, you fool, you damn fool," she said, "that normal people don't do things like that? Normal people don't hold fourteen-year-old girls down and take off their clothes and stick their fingers up in them."

"Don't talk like that," he said.

"Don't you see how crazy both you and Mother were? Are? Don't you see what you drove me to? Have you never seen it? Have you never thought about it?"

"But I never . . ."

"You never did anything? But you did it all. You drove me away from you and you drove me crazy and you made me, finally, after all was said and done, you made me, you," she stumbled to find the right words, "you sacrificed me. You sacrificed me to save the family honor and the family had no honor.''

''What do you mean?''

''You wouldn't let me have that baby. You made me go through hell. You almost killed me. Have you no idea what it was like? What I had to live with? What I still have to live with? Have you no idea?''

''I thought I was doing the right thing.''

''The right thing? You took me to that dark filthy place and I went in one way and came out another. I went in myself and came out another person. And you've never said a word about it. NEVER ONE WORD. You never talked about it. You never let me say a word. I've had to live with it all my life and I was innocent. I was. I swear I was.'' She was crying now, and she looked at him and he looked back at her and raised his hands and opened his palms. ''And still, now, you say nothing.''

''I thought I was doing the right thing,'' he said again. ''Believe me,'' he said and then neither said anything. For a long time they looked in opposite directions, lost in the coldness of betrayal and sadness, and when ten minutes was up, such a long time for silence when there was so much to say but no way to say it, Ervin asked, ever so politely and humbly, ''Now may I have my keys back? Please.''

''I feel great,'' Catherine said. ''Let's just lie here and talk. I saw this movie once about the Holocaust, you know the death camps, and it was really something. Just awful. It showed these starving people, real films of them, and I mean, how thin can a person get and not die, I mean, it was just awful, and there was this one woman, Faye Dunaway, I think, I'm not sure, but anyway, she had this plan to kill this Nazi guy because he was doing all this bad stuff to people, and then making her fuck him, only she had to keep letting him do it so she could catch him at the right moment. Did you see that one?''

"I think I missed it," he said. Catherine hopped out of bed. She still wore her boots. She drank a long pull from her warm Pepsi and then got back in bed.

"Anyway, I watch a lot of movies. I learn things from them. We've got cable, well, we used to, anyway, but it got took out, but when we had it I watched movies just all day long. It's cheaper than going to see them in town. They cost four dollars a ticket now. Do you have cable?"

"No."

"I loved it when we did. I saw this movie one time . . . are you getting tired? You look like you're falling asleep. It is late, isn't it? I can't believe how time flies. I just can't. Except when there's nothing to do, like in a waiting room or something, anyway, I'm tired, too. Sometimes I stay up all night and then feel fine the next day until about three and then I just crash. I mean, it's weird. It's like doing drugs and then coming off real fast. You just fall. Everything goes out of focus and like one minute you're fine and the next minute you're so tired you can't stand up."

"I think I better go," Robert said. "I thought earlier that I might stay a few days, but I think I better go."

"Are you really going to leave? Oh. I get it. You're going back to your wife. Right?"

"I think I better. She might be in trouble about now."

"How come?"

"She just might."

"It's the right thing to do. I can't go back to L.C. yet. I need to make him worry more. I think I'll just stay out a few more days. Do you have enough money to let me have a little to rent this room for a few more nights? I know I said I wasn't going to ask you for any, but you've been so nice to talk to and everything, I know you understand."

"I'll see how much I have."

"What are you going to tell your wife? You're not going to tell her about me, are you? Don't do that. When you love someone and find out they've been with someone else it makes you feel real bad. I know. One time this man I thought I loved did that to me. I was sixteen. He worked at Cone Mills in Hillsborough, where I worked, until it shut down, I was only working part-time, but anyway, he was real nice to me and then later on I found that he was sleeping with a friend of mine's mother and, shit, I can't tell you how that messed me up, for a little while, anyway. I broke up with his ass, but fast, let me tell you that.''

"I'm not going to tell her.''

"Good. I bet she's really beautiful. I can just imagine what she looks like. From what you said. Like those women in the ads. Does she look like that?''

"Sometimes.''

"I knew it. I knew somebody as nice as you would have a wife like that. How much are you leaving me?''

"How much is the room?''

"Fourteen. Plus tax.''

"Here's forty. Is that okay?''

"Oh, that's great. Now I can really work on L.C. He'll get so drunk he won't be able to go to the job for a week. I like a man what doesn't have to drink all the time. Do you think if I went back to school and studied art I could get a job like your wife's?''

"Why not?''

"I don't know. I can't make up my mind. I hate sitting behind a desk all day. Take a shower before you go home. You better. Sometimes you smell like the other person. That's a dead giveaway right there. Do you like me?''

"Very much. You are an interesting person.''

"I am. I really am, aren't I? It's all inside of me, though. I can't make it come out. I try to do all these different things, but I just can't. Like I can see myself doing all these different things, but I just can't make it happen.''

She followed him into the bathroom and leaned in the doorway while he ran the water waiting for it to get hot.

"You want me to wash you? I do it real well. It'll feel

good. You can't ever get your back clean unless somebody does it for you.''

"If you want.''

"Let me take my boots off. There. Just get in. Whew, that's hot. Good. Now turn around. You have a nice back. It's smooth. L.C. has pimples all over his. My back's smooth, like yours. I wish I had met you before you got married. If you weren't married, would you like me?''

"I like you anyway.''

"But would you like me enough to stay with me?''

"Maybe.''

"I know. It's hard to tell from just one night. We're different. Is it wrong for a Jew to fuck a Christian?''

"I'm not sure.''

"I hope you didn't commit a sin. One time these guys in school made this Catholic boy eat meat on Friday. They held him down and forced it in his mouth. I don't know what happened to him, though. I guess it'll be all right, because he didn't mean to, wouldn't it? I know it would. When people do things to you you don't want to happen, it's like they're not really happening, like you're not really doing it. It's like you're not really there. You know what I mean. It's like it's not a sin because they did it to him and he didn't want to do it, so he didn't do anything wrong. He's innocent.''

"That's true,'' he said. "All too true.''

"I know it is. Turn around and I'll wash you in the front too. Just close your eyes and lean your head back. That's right. You can wash me when I'm finished. Are you going straight home? What time is it, anyway?''

"It must be about two.''

"Ugh. Time to go to sleep. What are you going to tell her? I know. Tell her you got to town and you were real mad at her but after you walked around a little you realized how much you loved her and you had to come back. Wouldn't that work? I mean, just like in the movies. You can do it. And it'd be true, too. I can see it. Like, you run up to each other and kiss but you kiss each other real hard, it's a really wild kiss and it just goes all through your body and then you look at each other and walk off together. Do something like that, okay?''

"I don't know if I can."

"Yes, you can. Wash me now. See how big my nipples get? I told you they did. You don't have to wash me if you don't want to. I'm so little, though, it won't take long. Sometimes I wish I were taller, but really, I don't know if I'd be prettier or not. What do you think?''

"You're pretty just like you are."

"I knew you'd say that. I guess you better go now. Where'd you put the money?''

"Beside the chicken."

"Why don't you take what's left. I ate more than you did, anyway. The rest is yours. Take it. Take it to your wife, then she won't have to cook tomorrow. Is she a vegetarian?''

"No. Why?''

"I don't know. I just flashed on it, for some reason. I'd like to meet her, but I know I never will. It's funny, though. You make love with some woman's husband and then you want to meet her, like you want to talk with her or something. I've felt like that before. I don't know. It's crazy. What would you say? You couldn't tell her anything.''

"Curiosity, I suppose."

"You want me to dry you? No. I guess not. It's hard to dry somebody. Here, I'll take your clothes over by the heater so you can be warm when you dress."

She took the money and put it in her purse and then put on her skirt and blouse.

"I'm not going to sleep in these. It'll wrinkle them. I ought to wash them out after you go and hang them in front of the heater. I wish I had enough money to buy some new clothes. That'd make me feel better.''

"I just don't have any more."

"Oh, I know you don't. I just mean I wish I had some money. Period."

"I know the feeling."

"Yeah. Anyway, you're great. I'm really going to remember you. You even kissed me. I love a man to kiss me. I was with this man once and he was fucking me and I asked him to kiss me and he said he wouldn't but he would pull on my hair if I wanted. Stupid ass. It didn't even feel good. You're real sweet, though. Think about me sometime, will you?"

"I will."

"I guess I'll never see you again, but maybe I will. If I do and you see me and you don't want me to talk to you, just turn away. I'll understand."

"I wouldn't do that."

"Tell your wife how much you love her. Tell her you're sorry you ran out. Tell her whatever she did you know she loves you, too. Be sure to tell her you're sorry, though. That's important."

"I don't know if I can."

"Of course you can. You just say it. Anyway, it'll be true. You do love her. I can tell. She loves you, too. You can tell when a man has a woman who loves him. There's just something there you know you can't get to."

"I wish."

"It's there. Listen. Where'd you put the key? Oh yeah, I see it. Here. Hug me for just a second. Oh. That's nice. Now you better go. Don't slam the door. I hate to hear doors slammed. Close it quick. It's really cold. Bye, now."

"We're waiting for Mother," Sally said, and went toward the bedroom. "But I've got to lie down. I'm so tired I can't even see. I've got to get some sleep. Do what you want in here. Start the fire if you want. I'm dead," she said. "Just dead. Absolutely dead," she said and closed the door behind her and collapsed on the bed and Ervin stayed on the porch for a moment and then stepped into the yard and stood in the rain, getting colder and wetter by the minute but unable to think what to do, just stood there like a drunk, like a wino who had wakened after passing out on the sidewalk and found himself in a cold rain and rose up trying to get the two or three brain cells that still worked to tell him what next to do. He stood there like that, that empty of ideas, only the one Sally had given him current.

He carried in an armload of wood and started the fire, and after it was blazing, closed the damper in the pipe and the one on the stove and fell asleep on the couch. His sleep was troubled, this time not by cough medicine and pills but by the gauze unraveling from the plastic surgery he had done on himself to hide his confused and bitter face. Under that gauze all his skin was raw except for his erectile lips which had sucked the sweetness right out of his daughter and left her so empty she flew into the arms of anyone who would hold her, and left his wife so crazy she spent all her time trying to figure out what had happened or when it had happened or what next to do.

But you just don't know, Ervin thought, as he slowly woke up, how much I loved both of you and you can't know because this night would have never happened if you knew how much I've wanted to make things right, with both of you.

I can't even remember what it was, and I can't even tell you if I try, I don't even know when it was, that first moment with your mother, to whom I used to say, "We will never go anywhere without the other, we will never travel in a car, on a trip, or fly in a plane without the other because, what my dear, my darling little angel, would life be like without you, what, my sweet and precious little thing, would I have to live for without you." I don't even know, you see, when that first moment happened, when suddenly the charm that had sustained us was lost, struck down by what? I don't know.

I never knew, my daughter, he would have liked to have said, when it started and I never knew with you, either, not even that night, because it was before then and I don't know when, but you have to know I wanted back, I wanted to come back, to both of you but I got so messed up I couldn't even stand to touch another person, could do nothing but scream at you and your mother, faded away is what I did, so that the person standing in front of you squeezing your wrists with that ugly face was not me, it was not even a person I knew, but it was, he wanted to tell her as she lay on that bed so deeply asleep, the person I could not get away from, and I hated myself, I swear to you I did.

You must believe me when I tell you that your mother is not without blame. She has a side you have never seen. She saved it for me because whenever I wasn't what she imagined a husband should have been, whenever she didn't get her way, she was meaner to me than anyone had ever been, meaner than you had ever seen, but so subtly you couldn't know it, and it was she who taught me how to fight, how to go cold as death right in her arms just as she thought she had me back. She taught me that. It was the coldness, you see, that drove me away, that froze me out of your lives that made me go mad because she killed me, because she wanted me dead rather than like I was and she wouldn't let me go and so she killed me, you just don't know it, he wanted to tell her, you just never saw it because she saved it for me, so don't blame it all on me, don't, because it wasn't me acting that way and saying those things, it wasn't even a person I recognized.

The stove glowed red hot, orange really, and puffed smoke out the loose bolt holes and around the worn-out door gasket. Ervin opened the damper in the pipe and let the smoke up the chimney and went to the kitchen and opened the door to get some air and to cool off the place, it had gotten so hot during that awful sleep.

And in the other room, Sally was lost in her own sleep, lost in exhaustion, lost in confusion and worry that Robert might not come back, really might not, that everything she had tried so hard to make right, that the kindness and understanding she had found after so many awful nights in the skeletal arms of carnivorous beasts posing as men, as human, even, so far they were from knowing what she wanted, so far they missed she could hardly breathe while they took all they could from her and she gave it, not knowing what else to do, and with her worry and exhaustion she had the old elephant dream again, a stupid animal to dream about but there it was, ever since she was a child, the elephant-in-the-soap-dish dream and here it was again on this desperate night, the soap dish built into the tile wall and the naked little girl in the tub and the soap dish at eye level with the elephant coming, taking up the whole inside of the dish and swaying and rocking back and forth as it lumbered toward her and the trunk moving from side to side, and continuing toward her, a ridiculous dream, but there it was, year after year, and now again as she twitched and tried to get loose but was too tired and too lost to figure out even how to throw off the covers, just lay there and sweated and twitched.

And Ervin, in the kitchen, heard her moan and wanted to tell her, please forgive me, baby, please hold me, please let me take you in my arms and let's say it's all right, now, that it's over.

He so wanted it to be over. It hadn't been all his fault. He wanted to be forgiven for everything that he'd ever said or done that had been wrong. He wanted to get back to the better memories of himself, a long way to go back, maybe too far, maybe no way, and just as fast as the remorse had come, it left, as he felt pissed off at the goddamn mess he had made of his life and at all the goddamn people who had helped him do it, and the realization he might never get loose, especially with Margaret on her way up.

He turned the knob on Sally's door. He turned it carefully. The old mortised latch pulled back. Never in its hundred years of action had it reversed itself so slowly, so quietly, and he opened the door and with the light from the lamp behind him, he walked over to her bed and looked down at

Sally. He went to her dresser and carefully opened her top drawers and looked at her clothes and what he couldn't see he felt with his fingertips and turned to see if she had heard him and then went to the bed to see if she were really and truly asleep or just laying low, and decided she was gone, far gone, and he carefully, oh so carefully pulled back the top cover and then pulled back the wool blanket under which she slept curled up in the middle of the bed and he looked at her arms and her hands pulled against her breast and he put one knee on the bed and he leaned forward, right over her, keeping his balance with his other hand against the headboard as he reached for her hand, which held, still clutched but loosely now, his ring of keys, and as he slipped them loose she began to wake, to climb up from that deep sleep, struggling up, fighting to get awake like coming out of anesthesia, so lost she was, but brought back by the shock of another person's skin ever so lightly touching hers, and finally most of the way back, she smiled, still with her eyes closed and said, "Baby, I knew you'd come back," and she put her arms around Ervin's neck and pulled him down and then opened her eyes and shoved him back and rolled off the side of the bed and ran into the wall and spun around.

"WHAT IN THE HELL ARE YOU DOING?" she screamed. "WHAT ARE YOU DOING IN HERE?"

"I just wanted my keys," he said.

"TAKE THEM, DAMNIT," she said, "AND GET OUT OF HERE. I DON'T CARE WHAT YOU DO. JUST LEAVE!"

"I will. But let me talk with you first. Just for a minute."

"LEAVE. OUT."

He stopped just out of sight of the house and tried to throw up. He was trying to get rid of those hot dogs he had eaten on the way up, when he had pulled in at the sign which read 4-for-a-dollar, and which he had eaten even though they had tasted cheap and red and foul, but he couldn't throw up, so he just gagged and dripped spit and mucus and then got his breath and started out the driveway.

Margaret, at that moment, had just pulled in off the paved road and was starting down to confront this man. She was moving fast. She wanted to surprise him before he could think of some way out, before he would joke and cajole and worm his way out of what he had done, trap him in front of Sally, for once, where he would be exposed for the deceiver he really was, really had been, she thought, and Sally never knew it. She always took his side.

So with this in mind she cut off her lights and drove as fast as she could and still see the road and they met in a sharp curve halfway down the drive where his lights illuminated not the road or her car, but, because of the curve, the woods on the far side and they met in a collision so sharp and sudden Sally not only heard it but felt the concussion as well.

Margaret's lap-and-shoulder belt snapped tight as she was slung forward. The belt stopped her midway to the steering wheel. She sat in a daze until she focused on the camper and saw it was her husband.

"Ervin," she cried. "What happened?"

He was unconscious. His head was against the steering wheel and his body was jammed below it as if he'd been stuffed into the space between the bottom of the wheel and the floor. He was illuminated by the dome light as she opened the door.

"Are you all right?" she asked and he woke up, not to the words of the princess who found this frog and brought him back to life, but woke up because the bump on his head had only been that bad, thirty seconds' worth.

"You," he said. "I hit you?"

In his crushed-down position he looked as if he'd been born again, only this time with severe birth defects, no legs, no neck, a head coming out of the chest, but tilted back forever in a tortured position. "I really hit you?" he gurgled and then having already wet his pants from the force of the steering wheel against his stomach, threw up four bright red hot dogs that gagged from his throat and out his mouth like giant, bloody, oozing trichinal worms, swimming up, finally, after years of internal feasting.

"Oh hell," he said.

"Don't worry," she said. She ignored the vomit and the piss and hugged him. She had him, by God. She stroked his face and stroked his hair and told him to take it easy, that she would help him.

"Just get me out," he said, his voice different from anything she had heard. "Just help me, please," he said as she pulled his arm to get him to roll out sideways from between the steering wheel and the seat.

"Oh God," he moaned. "You're hurting me." He whined like a baby just as Sally ran up with a flashlight and the dog.

"What has happened?" she asked.

"We hit each other."

She shined the light on her father and leaned over to look and the smell retched in her stomach. She backed away and shined the light on the two vehicles. The car, with its brakes on, had hit low into the camper, which, higher than the car anyway, had ridden up over its bumper and had eaten into the front of the old Dodge as if it were taking a bite out of it, eating the lights and the grill and the top of the hood. The lights were smashed on the camper, as well, but the bumper on the big truck-chassied vehicle had absorbed most of the damage.

"Are you really okay, Mother?" she asked and shined the light up and down her body.

"I am, but help me with your father."

"I'm not going to touch him," she said.

"What?"

"You do it," she said and started off. "I'll get the house ready for you two. Just walk on down when you get him out."

"Sally," her father cried. "Sally. Sally. Sally, come back," he called.

The sound of her name coming from her injured father affected her like a magical incantation known only to members of a family, and she nearly lost her resolve.

"Come on," she told the dog, and they ran back to the house.

Mrs. Zilman punched her husband in the side and he turned over without waking. She kept a flashlight beside the bed and she shone it around the room.

She went downstairs. She passed the high-school-graduation portraits of her two children. The house seemed fine except her husband had left his cigar in the ashtray and the smell of the wet, chewed-up stub had fouled the air.

On the way back up the stairs she shone the flashlight at Robert's portrait and then hurried up and turned on the overhead light.

"Get up," she said.

"What?"

"Get up."

"Why?"

"Robert needs us."

"What do you mean. Did he call again?"

"No. But he needs us and this is one time we've got to do the right thing and help him out."

"But . . ."

"We've got to help him be strong."

"But he hung up on us."

"I don't know what that was all about, but I do know we've got to act fast. We're going up there."

"Now?"

"Yes. Now."

"Why don't we call first. Just to see if he's there."

"I don't want to do that."

"But we don't know what we're getting into."

"That's just it. Since he won't tell us anything, we can only assume the worst. We've got to find out what is happening up there and we've got to help Robert through this. He wouldn't have called us if he didn't want our help."

Dr. Zilman knew there was no stopping her but he was trying to slow her down a little.

"Can't we wait until morning?"

"No."

"Why not?"

"I can't sleep. I can't wait. I've got to know what's happening. He called me. Don't you see? He called us and asked us for help."

"But what about my patients?"

"We can be back by noon if we hurry."

"You want me to cancel the morning appointments?"

"Let's hurry," she said and soon they were on their way in the big Lincoln Town Car.

"I want some coffee," he said before they left town.

"Stop here," she said.

"That place?"

"I'll run in," she said, and she entered the Squawkin Walkin Chicken—take out or squawk right in—and bought two large coffees and two chicken biscuits.

"Sally," her mother said, "why did you walk away from us back there?"

They were in the kitchen. She and Ervin sat at the table and Sally stood with her back to the sink. Ervin's face was red and he had a bump on his forehead. The bump was blue and swollen and was bleeding. It bled until the ice pack stopped the bleeding and stabilized the swelling.

"That ice hurts as much as the bump," he complained to Margaret, who mashed the dripping towel with the ice against his head. "Just stop awhile. You're really hurting me."

"Not yet," she said, and looked at Sally. "Why?"

"Why? You should ask such a question. After what he did to you? Why didn't you just leave him there?"

"Because he needed my help."

"How did you get out, anyway?" Sally asked.

"Someone let me out," she said.

"See, Daddy. I know about it. I know you locked her in the bathroom."

"I had to," he said. "She was out of control."

"I was not," she said and mashed a little harder.

"Ouch."

"Just be still," she said. "You know who let me out?"

"Who?" Sally asked.

"I want Ervin to ask me. Guess who?"

"Okay. Who?"

"Angela."

He put his hands on her arm and pushed her back and looked at her.

"I don't believe it."

"But it's true," she said and she just glowed, like someone who had been keeping a secret for so long, so hard to keep it and not tell, and then finally gets to tell it, and there it is, the person's amazement, disbelief, there it is, the reward.

"How could she have possibly even known about it?"

"She didn't. She had come to find you and she heard me inside. And she let me out."

"I should have never come up here," he said and put his head down on his arms but forgot about the bruise.

"Damnit," he said.

"Don't cuss," Margaret said.

"What did she say?"

"She told me everything. And I told her that she wouldn't be seeing you anymore."

"You did? You told her that? And what did she say?"

"She heard me."

"Serves you right," said Sally. "That just serves you just right."

"Why are you so down on him?" her mother asked.

"Because we've had it out, and I was sure, I mean, at least I thought, that when you got up here you would have it out with him, too. I thought we were going to get all this cleared up."

"It is cleared up, isn't it, honey?" Margaret said to him.

"No. It's just starting."

"Oh no it's not. It's over. You and her are over. She'll leave town if I have anything to do with it."

"If I could just get out of here, I'd find out for myself what happened. Let me use the phone now, will you?"

"Not a chance," Sally said.

"Ervin," Margaret said, "you don't seem to grasp the situation. I drove up here to get you. To tell you it was all over. To bring you back."

"You won't learn, will you Daddy? He never learns. He's been pushing me and pushing you so long he can't stop himself. You can't, can you?"

"I can stop," he said.

"I always thought you two were in cahoots against me," Margaret said.

"You don't know the half of it. If I hadn't spent half the night crying, I'd be doing it again now. You just don't know."

"What is she talking about, Ervin?"

"I don't know."

"Where's Robert?" Margaret asked, startled that she had just realized he was nowhere in sight.

"He left. Long before Daddy got here. But after he found out he was coming."

"But why? Where did he go?"

"I don't know, but I can tell you why he left."

"Don't do that," her father said.

"Don't do what?" her mother asked.

"I will tell you because it's time you knew," she said and

she told her about the baby and the infections and the knotted-up tubes and the arthroscopic torture and the eggs that each month couldn't find their way past that wreckage and Margaret listened, absolutely astonished.

"And I never knew a thing," she said when Sally stopped talking. "How dare you," she said to Ervin, but in the calmest tone of voice, with finality, as if there could be no more proper and righteous thing to ask, but, how dare you, how dare you do this to her, to me, to us, behind my back and then live with it all these years, making the lie worse every day it went on.

"How dare you," she said again and threw the dripping-wet bundled-up ice compress on the table and stepped back. The ice spilled off the table and Sally cleaned it up.

"It was so long ago," he said. "It happened to a lot of people."

"It's not just that, Daddy. It is and was everything. Can't you see? It's all this pretending that everything's all right, that the way we've lived and the things we've done and the way you've treated Mother and the way you've dragged me into all the fights and trouble between you two, it's the pretending that it's all okay, that's what's so bad. Never owning up to it. Never admitting what's going on."

"I am just killed," her mother said. "I am just killed," she said again, both times to herself, but out loud.

"And that's why," Sally said, with her arms crossed, "you're not ever coming up here anymore. I mean it. Not without an invitation from me and Robert. Because your days of running over me and Mother are over. They're over because of your foolishness with Angie and they're over because finally, after all these years of my life, I have been able to tell you to leave me alone and mean it, because finally I have been able to look you in the eye and tell you all this. You owe me an apology and Mother an apology. You owe the whole damn world an apology."

"Just tell me what you want me to do," he said, seeing

no way out, after hearing once more this litany from his daughter, after seeing that he would never get away from Margaret and thinking that even if she hadn't scared off Angie, she would make life such hell on them he would never make it. "Just tell me what to do and I'll do it," he said.

"Answer me this," Margaret said. "Answer me truthfully."

"I will."

"Why did you stop sleeping in the same room with me? Why did you move out?"

"I've got to go to the bathroom," Sally said not wanting to be in the middle of that.

"I don't know," he said. "Why bring it up? It's been so long ago."

"You said you would answer me."

"I can't."

"But it started about the time all this happened with Sally."

"It did?"

"Don't you remember?"

"Not really."

"Did you wean off me because of what you did to Sally?"

"Maybe," he said. "I don't know."

"Was it that? Because I think it must have been, because I have been piecing it together while we talked and it was almost exactly at that time. I am sure of it. Was it the guilt? Is that what it was?"

"It must have been," he said, and as he said it Margaret turned away and her face changed as this amazing revelation surfaced, this unexpected gift from this night of such madness, this unexpected relief that it had not been her he was hating, but himself. A light bulb could not have come on in the cartoon image of her mind that would have been bright enough to illustrate the intensity of that revelation, the immediacy of the release that she felt, that it had not been her but something else.

''I think I understand so much more now,'' she said, and went over to him. ''I think I do.''

''I'm glad,'' he said.

''Things are going to be different now,'' she said.

''All right,'' he said.

''You don't have to see Angela anymore. You don't need to. Okay?''

''If you say so.''

''You'll never see her again. All right?''

''All right.''

''We won't have any secrets anymore.''

''All right.''

''This thing with Angie is over. I told her and now I'm telling you and I can see now what has happened and I can see now what to do. It may take a while, but we're going to have the life we have missed.''

''Okay.''

''When we get home, you will move back into our room.''

''I will.''

''I know you will. And then you're going to take me out to dinner twice a week. I've always missed that.''

''All right,'' he said.

''I want to go on a trip soon. A cruise. A long cruise.''

''Fine. If we can find the money for it.''

''We have it. We'll spend it.''

''All right.''

''We do everything together from now on. I see that was a big mistake, just letting you go off on your own so much. We go shopping together. We go everywhere together and when you retire, we're going to move up to the mountains.''

''I hate the mountains.''

''And I hate the coast. We're moving to the mountains. It's only fair. It's only fair that I get my way a little now.''

''Okay. What else?''

''I want a car. A new one.''

''What kind?''

"It doesn't matter. We'll decide that later. And you're going to start going to church with me. Every Sunday."

"All right."

"And not only that, I want you to join the men's discussion group."

"Is that all?"

"For now," she said. As Sally came back into the room, Margaret drifted along the waves of the comforting revelation that had come to her as if by gift, as if in necessity all needs will be met, as if, after the long suffering, there is the knowledge and strength to make life come out right, to forgive and forget and to go on.

At a little after three A.M. Mrs. Zilman took a folded piece of paper from her pocketbook. It was a hand-drawn map Robert had sent them years ago of how to get to the farm.

"Slow down," she said to her husband.

"I am slowing down."

"Stop," she said.

"Is this it?"

"I can't see. I can't read this."

"Let me see it," he said.

"You can't tell where the turnoff for the driveway is from this thing," she said.

"Let me take a look at it," he said.

"It says to turn right just past a burned-out house with the chimney still standing."

"It also says it's a half a mile from that intersection," he said.

They backed up and measured the distance and made the turn off the pavement and onto the red clay driveway. The red clay was slick as ice and the Zilmans slid into the ditch.

"Why'd you do that?" Mrs. Zilman asked.

"I certainly didn't mean to," he said.

"Now what'll we do?"

"I'll get us out."

He put the car in reverse and floored it and the back end of the car slid further into the ditch and began to dig down in the mud.

"Great," she said.

"Just be quiet," he said. "I'll put it in Drive-Two. That's for snow and ice."

He moved forward about half an inch. The tire made a sound like a siren. "We'll have to walk."

"In these shoes?"

"What can I do?"

"Let's go then."

"It's pitch dark," he said after he turned off his lights.

"I've got my flashlight," she said.

"You're shining it where you can see but I can't see a thing," he said.

"Just keep going."

As they walked, their shoes stuck to the red clay and every time they took another step a little more clay stuck to them, so that soon their feet felt heavy as anvils and Mrs. Zilman's shoes pulled right off.

"These are my new stockings," she said.

"My shoes are ruined," he said.

"What's that?" she asked, shining the light up ahead at a looming presence in the middle of the road.

"I don't know."

"It's a wreck."

"A wreck?"

"Look at that."

"How could you have a wreck in a driveway?"

"Don't look inside."

"Just keep going."

"It's none of our business."

"That's not their car."

"They don't have a camper either."

"Who else lives down here?"

"I don't know."

"Who else would?"

"I can't imagine," she said.

"You know he never was the same after he married her," he said.

"It started before then."

"It did?"

"Of course it did, you dope. That's why he married her," she said.

"Well, let's get calmed down now," he said. "We've got to play this right."

"I'll play it right. Don't you worry about that."

"We don't know what we're going to find," he said.

"You may not," she said. "But I'm going to find my son."

The dog heard them and barked and Sally came out and saw a person with a flashlight. Ervin stepped out beside her.

"Who is that?"

"It might be Robert," she said.

"Oh. It probably is. He couldn't get by the wreck."

"Robert?" she called.

"He's not there," Mrs. Zilman whispered.

"It's the Zilmans," her husband called.

"Oh no," Sally said and thought, This is the night, this must be the night the world will end because what else can happen to me and what are they doing here anyway, and Ervin went back inside and told Margaret who it was and they prepared to meet these people for the first time ever.

"We're drenched," Mrs. Zilman said.

"I never knew you lived so far back," her husband said.

They charged in with four wet, red clubfeet, stumped onto the porch and right into the kitchen where they saw the Neals.

"Who are you?"

"We're the Neals," Ervin said and extended his hand.

"Who are the Neals?" Mrs. Zilman asked her husband, forgetting they were there and she could ask them.

"We're Sally's parents," Margaret said.

"That's impossible. Her name isn't Neal," Mrs. Zilman said, losing her resolve to stay calm and be nice in the face of this unexpected and disturbing development.

"Her name used to be Neal," Ervin said.

Sally came back into the room with newspapers and towels.

"I don't understand what you're doing here," Mrs. Zilman said.

"It's a strange time for you to drive up, as well," Ervin said.

"But we had to," she said.

"Why?" Sally asked.

"Because Robert called us."

"He told us what was going on," her husband said.

"I see we were right to come," she said, looking at the reinforcements on the other side.

"Why did Robert call you?" Sally asked.

"You should ask such a question," Mrs. Zilman said. "And your parents right there."

"Now, dear," her husband said.

"I don't know what you mean," Sally said.

The Zilmans hovered beside the woodstove. Mrs. Zilman took off her clear plastic rain hat and shook it and the drops sizzled on top of the stove and steam rose and the bad smell of warm, wet wool drifted across the room as her skirt began to heat up and smoke and Sally looked at it and thought, I hope she catches fire, the damn old bitch.

"What do you mean, her parents right here?" Ervin asked.

"What about it, Sally?" Mrs. Zilman asked.

"I don't know what you're talking about," she said.

"You won't get the farm," she said.

"What?"

"Not all of it, anyway."

"What does she mean?" Margaret asked Ervin, holding his arm.

"The laws of divorce divide things equally in this state," Mrs. Zilman said. "Especially when there are no children."

"What divorce?" Margaret asked.

"What are you talking about?" Sally asked. "You mean Robert said . . . ?" she began to ask.

"He didn't have to say it. We could tell."

"What is this all about?" Ervin asked Sally.

"Did he really talk to you about it?" Sally asked.

"Of course he did. He wanted our advice."

"It's not possible."

"Then what are we doing here at four in the morning and how did we know to come up?"

"Where is Robert?" Sally asked.

"He'll be here," Mrs. Zilman said.

"He will?" her husband asked.

"He couldn't have called you. He just couldn't have," Sally said. "And if he did, he wouldn't have asked you to come up. He just wouldn't have," she said and then thought, Could he have done that? For spite? Would he really have done that? She wasn't sure, then, because things had broken too abruptly, and because she wasn't sure she said to both sets of parents, but especially to the Zilmans, who seemed at this moment far worse than her own, "I would like all of you to leave. This is my house," she said, "mine and Robert's, you see, and I would like all of you to leave right this minute, rain or no rain."

"If it's part Robert's then," Mrs. Zilman said, "I'll just wait until he tells me to leave his part."

"You'll leave when I tell you to and I'm telling you now," she said and towered over the spindly woman who weighed, after a lifetime of diets, 105 pounds.

"We won't," she said and stuck her nose up in the air and crossed her arms.

"YOU WILL," Sally yelled and pulled her across the room so hard it took Ervin Neal, that Korean War soldier and veteran of a lifetime of domestic conflict, to stop Sally to stop Sally from absolutely slinging the woman right out the door.

"Hold on, Sally," he said and pulled her loose.

"Let go of me."

"She's crazy," Mrs. Zilman said.

"Don't, Sally," Margaret said.

"I knew it," Mrs. Zilman said. "She's crazy and violent."

"No one's leaving, anyway," Ervin said to Sally, who faced all four of them like a wolverine backed into a corner. "No one can leave because the driveway's blocked."

Sally locked herself in the bathroom and left the parents with each other.

Robert drove as fast as he could and still stay on the driveway. He knew it had gotten so slick that, as on snow, he had to keep moving because once stopped, it would be nearly impossible to get moving again. Up ahead he saw his parents' big Lincoln in a ditch.

The Zilmobile, he thought. Holy shit, what's this all about and he zoomed by it and saw no one and looked back to the road just in time to lock his wheels and slide to a stop behind the Dodge and the camper.

Uh oh. Real trouble now.

He began the longest walk of his life. It took longer and was more difficult than being born. It was worse than walking down the hall alone and into the first-grade class by himself when he was six. It was longer than walking down the hall with everyone else in class on his way to the principal when, in high school, he had thrown a pie at the back of a teacher's head—somehow it was going to be so funny, the dare to do it like a drug, the absolutely sleepless night before, and as the pie left his hand and sailed toward the back of that sixty-five-year-old woman's head in her last year at the school, the pie and the gasp from the students and that old gray-hair full of dandruff flaking onto the shoulders of her dress, day in and day out, did she ever wash her hair, the thrill of the whole stunt suddenly collapsed and if he could have gotten that pie back he would have given anything to do so—longer than that walk to be suspended for three days, the only time in his life he had ever gotten into trouble in school, and the other guys who put him up to it still laughing, while he sat at home grounded forever, longer than the walk to get married in the Baptist church where that wild Neal girl had come home to, bringing with her that poor boy who must have known nothing, but nothing, about her at all, and he finally came to his house, not knowing what he would find but certain and determined if there was a way and she would still have him, to rescue Sally from this trouble.

"Where's Sally?" he asked.

"Robert," his mother said, and rushed forward, as if to protect him from those Neals. "We came as fast as we could."

"What the hell for?" he asked and pushed by her.

"Robert," his father said, and "Robert," Ervin said and offered his hand, "we're glad you came back," he said, blocking Robert from going through the door, and Robert said, looking down at his offered hand and then at his face, "I'm not talking to you. Get out of my way," he said, and slammed the door in their faces and left them with each other, trapped like litigants in a courtroom, forced to face each other after telling every piece of dirt they knew about the other, like members of a tour group trapped on a ship at sea after falling out with one another so badly they couldn't stand the sight, much less the sound, of the other, no way out and no way in, like that they sat, the wives holding the husbands' hands, each looking as married as could be, a little contest going on to see who could act the better wife in this generation where men were men and women were theirs, and the husbands sullen and tough and not looking across the room, mostly wanting to get home and get some sleep and let life go on as usual, goddamn children, it was her idea to have them, and while Robert searched for Sally the tension just grew, until something had to happen, someone had to talk.

"If, uh, you don't mind," Ervin said, "I'm going to try to get a wrecker out here now and tow us loose and pull your car out of the ditch. If you don't mind."

"Fine. Fine. That'd be fine," the dentist said.

"Someone might come out this time of night, even in this weather, for enough money."

"I'll pay," the doctor said. "Whatever it costs."

"I think the camper's okay. I think we can drive it home."

Robert knocked on the door. Sally did not answer.

"It's me, baby," he said.

They held each other for a long time.

"You didn't tell your parents you wanted to divorce me, did you? You couldn't have."

"Never. I never said a word about it."

"Where have you been?"

"Just messing around. I couldn't stay away, though. I thought I might let things settle down and stay away for a few days, but I couldn't stay away from you, baby. I just couldn't."

"Don't leave me again," she said.

"I won't."

"I want to be alone with you. I want them gone. Can't you do something to get them out of here?"

They went back. He had his arm around her shoulders. She had her arm around his waist.

"We've got to get your cars out of the driveway," he said.

"I've already called a wrecker," her father said. "He's on his way."

"Then let's go meet him and see what can be done," Robert said.

"My shoes are ruined," the dentist said.

"I'll take you back out in the truck after we get the road cleared."

"Be careful with the Lincoln."

"Don't worry."

The wrecker came. Ervin and the driver and Robert worked together and pulled the Lincoln back to the paved road. They pulled the wrecked vehicles apart and started the engines. Except for some of the lights and the grilles and the fenders, they worked fine. The radiators had not been punctured and the steering was all right.

"Can I talk with you a minute, Robert?" his mother asked.

"No."

"But I thought, when you called . . ."

"That was a mistake."

"It wasn't."

"Just forget that happened and get in the truck and let's get out of here."

The Neals rode out to the paved road, sitting on the wheel housings in the truck bed, and the Zilmans rode in the cab.

"Are you really going back to her?" his mother asked.

"Of course. I never left. I don't know what the hell you came up here for, anyway."

"Don't talk to us like that," his father said.

"You're like a bunch of vultures."

"That's enough of that, you hear me," his father said.

"Every chance you get, all the time I've been with her, you've tried to make me feel like shit for marrying her."

"Don't cuss around your mother."

"Shut up," he said.

"We sure made a mistake," his mother said.

"You sure did."

"She's the best thing that ever happened to me. Every minute of my life with her has been better than anything that went on before."

"That's not true and you know it isn't," his mother said.

"You wouldn't have run away and called us if it were true," his father said.

"Just forget that, I said."

"You want us to just forget you?" his father asked.

"That's fine with me."

"All right, then," he said.

"Robert," his mother said.

"Just get out of the truck," he told them.

The Zilmans left without saying goodbye to the Neals. The Neals stood an awkwardly long time in front of Robert, waiting for him to speak, or to think of what to say.

"I guess Sally will tell you everything," Ervin said.

"Try not to think badly of us," Margaret said.

"We did our best."

"We love you. Both of you."

"We really do."

"Shake my hand, at least. You'll do that, won't you?" Ervin asked.

"Sure," Robert said.

"We're going, then. Tell Sally we'll call her when we get home."

"Take care of our little girl, now, you hear?" Ervin said.

"I always have."

"We're going, then."

"Go," Robert said.

"We'll call you."

"Around supper."

"You two get some sleep."

"We can make it," Margaret said. "We'll sleep after we get home."

"We're a bunch of tough old buzzards," he said. "We've done without sleep before."

"Bye, now."

"Call us if you need anything. Anything at all," she said, and as soon as they turned to go to their vehicles, Robert climbed back in the truck.

"There is nothing left of me," Sally said. "I have never, never, ever spent such a night."

"Me either."

"You're not going to work tomorrow. I mean, today. Surely you're not."

"Are you?"

"No way. I've got to get some sleep. I just have to."

"But what happened? What happened with your father and how did your mother end up here, I mean she can't even drive and when did my parents arrive? You've got to tell me."

"I can't. I don't want to even remember it."

"I can't wait. I've got to know all about it."

"I'll tell you. Later."

They rested and after they rested, they cleaned up, and bathed in their victory.

"We ran them off. We really did, didn't we?"

"You better believe it," he said. "I told my mother to shut up. I've been wanting to tell her that my whole damn life."

"And I think Daddy's going to leave us alone from now on."

"I hope so. But tell me. Tell me all about it," he said and they put on warm pajamas and got under the covers and held on to each other and she told him. It was the right time for everything to come together, for all to be forgiven, for the celebration of freedom from the humiliations and decadence of the past, for their future to glow in that eerie light that surrounded the departing alien craft as the two good people of earth send the creatures away, for the music's crescendo, the crashing of the waves, it was the right time, no doubt about it, for all of this to come together, but it did not happen.

Like shell-shocked and battle-fatigued soldiers who hear the story of their near death once more, like the mother reliving the death of her child as she had watched her teeter and then fall from the roof, unable to reach her, like that, it just brought it all back again to Robert, and he turned mean as his exhausted system simply overloaded with the confusion and disappointment, and he said, he even heard himself saying it as if he were not, heard himself saying it while he was thinking that he shouldn't, most definitely shouldn't be saying this, he said, "But all in all, after everything's said and done and we've run them off, I've still got to live with what I know, with being number you-know-what," he said, ashamed the very second the words were out and like the pie sailing through the air, too late now to take them back.

"Oh no, baby, no. Why did you say that?" she asked.

"I don't know. It just came out."

"How could you?"

"I didn't mean it."

"But you did."

"I don't know."

"You are a fool. You really are," she said and turned away. "After all this, after the fight I put up for us, after all this you come back with the ridiculous number business."

"It just came out."

"Oh baby," she said. "I can't stand it. It means it's going to be there forever."

"No it doesn't."

"It does, damn you," she said and got out of bed.

"Hey."

"Hey nothing. You better get that out of your head and I mean now."

"Or what? I mean, is this, like, a threat, or a challenge, or what?"

"It's just good sense, that's all. It's just what's right."

"Look. It's hard to get it all balanced out. It's like, I don't know, it's like you think about something one way for a long time and then you have to think about it another way and it's hard."

"Don't start that crap again," she said. "It's not my fault if you had some idealized version of me in your mind. I never pretended anything."

"But you did. You pretended it all."

"I never pretended a thing."

"Well, it seemed to me you did."

"You're the one who pretended." She walked to the window. "You're the one who pretended I was something no one ever is. Pure and innocent and fresh off the shelf where I'd been waiting like a little doll for you to come along and pick up. I mean, what shit. Give me a break. Can you believe anyone would be like that? Can you believe yourself? That's what we ought to be talking about. Really. Isn't it? Think about it. What kind of fool were you anyway?"

"You've gone too far now. You just have."

"No. I haven't, because I can see it now and I hate what I see. It's just too much. It's the whole thing again. I see that you thought of me one way, and now that it's not as you thought, I'm a fallen woman, and that's exactly," she said, and thought, dear God how could it be, "that's exactly what my father did to me. It's just too much. That is exactly what happened. After I became a fallen woman in his eyes things were never the same again. He couldn't ever think about me in the same way again."

"It's not the same," he said.

"But it is. This whole night, this whole scene, is like a night from my parents' house," she said and her anger broke into despair. "I can't take it. It's not my fault. Suppose I was coming home from work and I was raped. What then? I mean, tell me. Would that be my fault, too? Would you never be the same with me after that? One minute I'm yours and the next minute I'm not. One minute I'm pure and sweet and all yours and the next minute I'm not. How could that be? You're just like him. How could I have done this to myself? How could I, how could I, how could I? You're mad at me because you found out something about me you didn't like, something about me that didn't fit with the way you thought women are supposed to be, or wives are supposed to be. That's what happened to him. With me and with Mother. How perverse can you get? I'd just as soon be dead," she said and pointed at him and said, "Please leave me alone for a little while. Please. I am going to bed."

He left the room and quietly closed the door and boiled a pot of water for tea and took a sip and then lay on the couch exhausted and soon they were both asleep, even as the sun came up and the rain stopped, they were both asleep, even as the new day began and their chance with it, Robert and Sally slept, separated now by so much more than merely walls.

Ervin and Margaret parked their banged-up vehicles in the driveway. It was eleven A.M. Twenty-four hours earlier, Margaret had just earned her driver's license. Sixteen hours earlier she had been locked in the bathroom.

"That'll give the neighbors something to talk about," she said, taking his arm and glancing back at the wrecks.

"We'll get them fixed tomorrow," he said.

"Should we get the old car fixed or trade it as is for my new car?" she asked.

"Oh. Well. Let me think about it."

"Take today and tomorrow off," she said and he called in sick. He was sick.

"I'm going to stay on that diet," she said.

"That'd be nice," he said. He was so disoriented and uncertain as to where he actually stood with her and with Angie and with himself, he couldn't think. He was like a man who'd come out of shock therapy, and who'd then had a prefrontal lobotomy thrown in for good measure.

"We might take this tour here," she said and pointed to a brochure.

"Okay."

"Are you rested now?"

"A little."

"Do you want to go to bed?"

"No. Nope. Not at all. I'm awake now. The day's begun. Might as well stay with it."

"Then call her."

"Call who?"

"Angela."

"Not now."

"Now."

"But I've got a headache."

"I'll get you some aspirin."

"Let's just forget about it. Let it go. Let it just fade away. How about it?"

"I want you to call her. I want to hear you tell her it's over."

"I can't."

"Now, Ervin," she said and began to get rough. She squeezed his arm and looked him in the eye.

"Just calm down."

"Hold this phone in your hand," she said and she got the telephone directory and dialed her number.

"She won't be there. She'll be at work."

"After last night I bet she takes off, too."

Angie answered. "Is that you Ervin? You sound funny. Are you at work?"

"I didn't make it."

"Where in the world have you been?"

Margaret picked up the extension.

"Who's that on the phone? I heard someone," Angie said.

"It's me," Margaret said.

"Who is that, Ervin?"

"It's Margaret."

"It's his wife," Margaret said.

"What's this about?"

"Ervin has something to tell you."

"Why don't you let him talk?" Angie asked.

"Go on."

"Well, Angie, Margaret wanted me to call you . . . you see, I had this wreck. . . ."

"Forget the wreck," Margaret said. "Just tell her."

"Well, we had a real long night up there."

"Where?" Angie asked.

"At Sally's."

"Oh. Is that where you went?"

"And lots of things kind of came to a head, and it seems that we're going to, well, it seems that we've decided to stay together after all."

"What are you trying to do, Ervin Neal?" Angie said. "Why are you calling me with her on the other line and telling me this? Don't you have enough guts to be honest about it and do it on your own?"

"Well . . ."

"You don't, do you? It's all been a big act. And I've been a fool again, believing everything I'm told, just like that crippled business. What a laugh. You want me to tell her that? How about it, Ervin?"

"What?" Margaret asked.

"I don't know what she's talking about."

"Oh yes you do. And another thing. You can't break up with me. I was finished with you last night. I don't need a man like you. I don't need a man who's got something like her around his neck," she said and hung up.

"She's a bitch," Margaret said.

"Are you happy now?"

"I am. You did the right thing."

Ervin walked toward the door.

"Wait a minute. What's she talking about, crippled? What was that?"

"I don't know. She's just making up things."

"Where are you going?"

"Outside. May I?"

"What for?"

"I just want to go out."

"Where are you going?"

"In the yard."

"All right. But don't go far."

"I won't."

He put on his lined jacket and, like an old man being let out the front door of the nursing home for a stroll, walked into the yard and then stood there, not sure what next to do.

He shuffled over to the car. He looked at the damage. He looked at the front of the camper. If he called the insurance company, his rates would go up. Maybe Wart could fix them. Maybe he could get used parts and fix them.

He walked down the drive toward the road.

"Where are you going?" he heard her call from the front door.

"To check the mail," he said and pointed to the box on the post at the end of the drive.

"You know it's not here yet. You know it doesn't get here this early."

"Oh. Yes," he said and started back.

"Stay around the house. Go in the backyard and stay there."

He shuffled in that direction. It sounded like she had said, "Go in the backyard and play there," and he thought, Well, maybe she'll fence it in and let me play back there all by myself someday.

Margaret picked up the phone and dialed Evelyn, the woman from her church who'd been driving her on Sunday morning. She looked out the window while she talked.

"And we're taking a cruise, too."

"You are?"

"Yes. Two whole weeks. No house to clean, no meals to cook, no clothes to wash. I'm so excited."

"But why all of a sudden," Evelyn asked, "after all these years? I've never known you two to even take a trip together."

"Oh, nonsense. We always have. It's just that as of late we've been saving up for something special. And here it is."

"Second honeymoon?"

"Something like that," Margaret said.

Ervin shuffled around the backyard until the sun went behind some clouds and he got cold and he came back and sat with her in front of the television and picked up a magazine and looked at the pictures.

When a person burns up in a fire, he thought, remembering a mystery he had read, the police check to see if there is smoke in the lungs. If there is no smoke, then they know the person was dead before the fire and the fire was set to cover the murder.

Therefore, he thought as he looked at the pictures, if a person was drugged unconscious and then locked in a room and then burned up in a house fire, the smoke would be in the lungs and everything would look right.

When you start a fire, he thought, you need to make it start in just one place, and have some frayed wires or something like no screen in front of the fireplace and a log rolls out onto the carpet and sets the house on fire.

When a fire starts in just one place, it doesn't look as if its been set, especially if there's not much insurance and the person who got burned up was getting along fine, according to everyone, getting along better than ever, getting along so well, wasn't it a shame for such a thing to happen just when they were doing so well.

But what if the person doesn't burn up all the way and even with the smoke in the lungs the drugs are discovered during the autopsy?

That's a problem, like the problem with hiring someone to kill someone, to shoot them, you have the problem of the killer telling just one person about it and that person gets picked up for something and then squeals to make a deal and then they trace the phone calls all around and even with an alibi and the money in cash and all that, the trail leads back to you.

"Come have lunch," she called.

"I'll be right there."

* * *

Sally awoke in bed, just as the sun was setting. She opened her eyes and from where she lay, without raising her head, saw a spectacular giant red sun, bigger than usual, as if while she slept the earth had moved closer to the sun. It was just beginning to set below the tops of the pines, the only thing green in the winter horizon. She lay still. She listened for Robert. She did not hear him and she thought, If he will talk to me, I will talk to him.

After a while longer in bed, she went in the opposite direction from where he lay and washed up. She was hungry and had not eaten, she figured as she scrubbed her face, really, since the night before, so long ago now.

She walked through the living room and Robert was on the couch, reading a catalog. He did not look up and she walked by and opened the refrigerator and tore the duck in half and heated it and because she had cooked it twice now, the skin was extra-crispy. She threw the carcass to the dog and gave the cat a tough, hairy piece of skin she hadn't been able to chew.

She went back into the living room and stopped directly in front of him and he kept on reading. He was now reading the classified ads from yesterday's newspaper. After ignoring her for a moment, he looked up and then past her and chewed on a fingernail and slumped on the couch sullen, not ready to talk.

She went in the bedroom. He heard her opening and closing drawers. She came through the living room on her way upstairs. The first time she came through she had a pile of his clothes, and then his shoes and the stuff off the top of his dresser and then everything from his side of the closet and finally a pillow and two extra blankets.

She moved him upstairs. The stalemate began.

Part III

The HOSTAGE CRISIS

Thirteen

In Wilmington, on a narrow residential street in a house with wrecked cars in the driveway and backwards doorknobs inside, in the dark of the moon, in the cloudy night, Ervin and Margaret lay down together.

Across town, in the apartment complex with the rusty iron stairways and cracked concrete balconies and wobbly wrought-iron railings, behind the hollow-core door with the hole punched through the inside layer of veneer, Angie and a stranger lay down together.

In the first house, in the shared bedroom, with the door closed and the heat from the two bodies rank as rotten meat in the sun, Ervin's gonads tried to pull loose and run out of the room.

And back across town, in the room built out of metal studs and busted sheetrock with no insulation, and a brown rug stained and worn nearly smooth on the concrete-slab floor, and an orange sofa with tufted upholstery frayed and torn by years of nervous picking and pulling while game shows screamed laughter down the throats of tenants, men and women pale as the flesh-colored walls around them, in this room, on the couch with human legs hanging off one end and another set of legs slung out to each side, all four legs

217

suddenly pulled up in ecstatic contraction as Angie and the strange young man tore into each other.

Back in the first house, Ervin was frozen solid as a sea of ice, blinded, strangled by the scream he had had to swallow and listening as the great white body of his wife shifted in bed and swam slowly toward him.

Across town again, empty eyes stared down the holes of hollow sockets. "Fucked her eyes clean out of her head," the strange young man thought and bared his teeth in a bony grin while she looked up at the face, bitten and chewed and scarred into the skinless face of a blood-red hockey mask. "Don't wake my daughter," she whispered as the man gurgled like death behind the mask. "I wouldn't want her to know about this," she whispered, and pulled him down again with her eyes closed while the dream of lost loves and perfect, beautiful lives flickered like an old film run far too many times, faded, distant, confused, and spliced together now after each painful break in such a way that nothing was clear anymore, only the memory of what might have been when it had all begun so long ago for this Angela of the sweet and innocent and elusive dream.

And yet, across town, where the other woman refused to give up the same dream of so many years, the comic flight of her husband's madness flapped against her like the wings of a bird as she paused in that long journey across the bed, a distance measured in years of determined, faithful forbearance.

She swam across the bed, undulating beneath all that flesh like a dolphin, sleek and powerful.

Ervin's gonads jerked back and tried to hide from the cold female hand creeping toward them.

"I can't," Ervin mumbled.

"What's that, honey?" she asked.

"I said . . . it's late."

"It's not too late," she said and rolled on top of him. "Oh, honey," she said.

Bamboo under the fingernails was nothing compared to this. The water torture, a drop of water every three seconds on the forehead of the bound prisoner, was nothing compared to this. This death was more like the death of the brittle glass catheter, shoved up oh so slowly, and then shattered. This death was more like the murders going on every day behind the locked doors of pleasant-looking dwellings where each person holds the other prisoner until he finally agrees to talk, finally gives in, but a little too late, arms and legs gone, faces strained beyond recognition. Who is this? Who are you? they ask, suddenly looking up from the table with astonishment and horror at what they have done to one another.

"Oh honey," she said again the next morning as they had breakfast.

"More tomahto juice?" she later asked in a queenly voice.

"Of course, my dear," he said, and sucked it down, making his mouth into a long straw like the proboscis of a mosquito. "But of course," he said and smiled at her with his long, grinning tube of a mouth, while his lips, set like the nostrils on the end of the trunk of an elephant, quivered and rolled back in a juicy, red smile of obscene delight.

After breakfast, Margaret called Sally, who was near the phone staring out the window, so that she answered it almost before the first ring.

"And we're going down to get the new car today," she told her daughter. "And guess what else?"

"I don't know."

"We are going on that cruise. For Valentine's Day."

"That's good."

"We're going to Bermuda." There was talking in the background. "That was your father. He made a joke about Bermuda shorts."

Ervin squatted in front of the television watching nothing in particular but straining to hear it, nevertheless. It was not exactly the strain of squatting with a sore leg, or the strain of listening with the sound turned down that made his face turn red. It was more likely the difficulty of the problems ahead.

It was difficult, for instance, to throw someone overboard without being seen. It was difficult to claim accidental death from choking when you're caught with your fist down the victim's throat. It was difficult to claim that the steering linkage on a brand-new car had come loose and that somehow all the cotter pins holding all the nuts to the tie rod ends had just let go, at full speed down the interstate, so that both front wheels suddenly turned sideways.

"I'll call again, soon," Margaret said.

"Don't bother," Sally said.

"Oh I will. It's no bother."

"Good-bye."

"Your father says hello."

"Uh huh," Sally said.

"Tell Robert we love him."

"Good grief, Mother. Just hang up. Go buy your car. Hang up, all right?"

Robert looked from the couch when Sally hung up the phone but she neither looked back at him nor said anything. She just left the room and closed the door.

Fourteen

Life goes on, but it will never be the same again, Robert thought as he faced the second day at home with Sally, neither person talking, neither person leaving, neither person daring so much as to step out of the house. The one still inside might lock the doors. The one left inside might appear at the window, arms loaded with the cherished possessions of his or her half of the marriage, books bought before the marriage, furniture from the family house, heirlooms from the family history, where madness, if it existed, and anger and hatred and betrayal remained buried with the white, shining countenance of the silent ancestors.

It was day two of this private hostage crisis, where no dogs barked, no cats cried, and where the damaged hearts of the hostages themselves beat with the erratic murmurs of sadness.

It was difficult to actually go that long without talking to one another. A few hours was one thing. Two entire days confined together was another. Thoughts of reconciliation and anger surfaced ready to be released. The silence continued. Robert suffered in the privacy of his stubbornness. Sally suffered in the rarefied air of hurt feelings. Finally, at suppertime, that moment of domestic reckoning even in the households of silence—Will he eat? Will he eat with me?

Will we eat together and pay homage to the relationship? Will she cook anything I like? Will she cook anything at all? Will we sit down together in at least a momentary truce?—Robert cracked and started talking.

"I see you're not washing the dishes," he said.

She didn't answer. All around her the pots and pans and dishes were scabrous with dried food.

"Well, I'm not going to wash them," he said.

She found a clean aluminum pot and dumped a can of ravioli into it.

"Where'd you find that?" he asked. "You've been hiding food, haven't you? I looked everywhere for that. It wasn't on the shelf."

She stirred it and lowered the flame.

"What are you doing, keeping it in your room now?"

She stirred the ravioli again. It was easy to let the pasta burn and stick to the bottom if one didn't watch it carefully.

"I don't have to talk either," he said. "I can go back to not talking. You're not proving anything by staying at it longer than me."

He opened the refrigerator. There wasn't much left. It had begun to snow outside. It if snowed much, and it stayed as cold as predicted, it would be impossible to get out of the driveway. The state roads wouldn't be plowed until the snow stopped falling.

"It's snowing, anyway," he said, and took out the last slices of bologna, a jar of mustard and the last Pepsi.

"I hate baloney," he said and rolled up one of the slices and dipped it into the mustard and took a bite. "Beef lips, beef hearts and God only knows what else."

She took the pan off the stove and went into the other room. It was time for the evening news. There was no report on the two people holding each other hostage in the backwoods of Chatham County.

"You haven't phoned in at work," he said. "You're going to get fired."

Sally blew on a steaming square of ravioli that sat neatly on her spoon. It was nice to get them out of the pot whole. It was neater. It was like a little sandwich one ate with a spoon.

"I wonder why they haven't called for you," he said. She had unplugged the phone.

"See, I mean, you think you're the only one with problems, or something. You're not. Everybody comes from crazy families. I mean, I didn't get it, you know, like you, but it was bad enough."

She set the pot on a book to keep it from burning her. She was wearing shorts. The house was warm. There was plenty of wood inside in the bin.

"People never know what they're getting into. The whole thing reminds me of this man who broke into a meat-packing plant and stole two unmarked boxes of frozen meat. These big white institutional boxes, you know. The owner of the plant said the man was going to be surprised when he thawed them out and opened them up, because he had stolen two boxes of beef assholes."

He looked at her for a reaction. She watched the news.

"See, they use everything from the cow. The lips, the nose, the assholes, everything. I don't know what they use them for, but they do," he said. "Imagine going to jail for stealing assholes. Imagine what your name would be forever after that. You'd never live it down."

She put another whole square in her mouth. It was Chef Boyardee. She had been eating it since she was a child. It was as good as ever.

"One time when I was about twelve we had tongue one night. My father loved tongue. To him it was a special event. My mother brought it in on a platter. There, sitting right in front of us, was this pink, grainy slab of meat in the shape of a giant tongue. It gagged me something terrible. I couldn't swallow it. It just fluttered around in my mouth as if it were my own tongue I was trying to swallow."

She put the pot on the floor. She went back into the kitchen. She returned with a glass of ice water.

"See, we ate a sit-down meal every night. Every night at six. Terrible tension every night that we wouldn't begin right on the dot. That the food wouldn't be perfect. Everyone had to eat whatever was served. My father told my little sister the night of the tongue, if she threw up she'd have to eat the vomit."

He rolled up another piece of bologna and dipped it into the mustard jar and ate it. It wasn't bad, but it certainly wasn't good, either.

"See, he meant well, but he just didn't know how to go about it. My little sister started crying and had to leave the table. At least she didn't have to eat the tongue."

Sally turned to another channel. The "MacNeil–Lehrer Newshour" was on. Four people were being interviewed about a problem. From the camera work it looked as if these combatants were being interviewed from all over the world, in the country of their own origin, and not, as they were, sitting side by side at the same table in the studio.

"See, parents mean well. They just don't know what they're doing, and they don't know how to say what they know they should say. Some of them try to gag you with a piece of tongue. Others do it in other ways."

She scraped up the tomato sauce from the bottom of the pot. She had eaten the entire fifteen-ounce can. She set it down again and changed channels once more.

"See, I've been thinking. You can't blame them, I guess, even if they do something horrible to you. You can't blame them because they're your parents and whatever they did, it was part of something that was a part of your family, you know, part of your own craziness, I guess I'm saying. But when other people find out about it, it's bad. It's real bad. It's like someone else's dirt is so much dirtier than your own."

It was snowing hard now. It was predicted to be one of the biggest snows ever. The schools would be closed. Everyone would stay home. In the quiet of a snow you can hear someone calling from far away.

"It's like going in someone else's bathroom, you see," he said, babbling on out of control. "Or in a public restroom. One hair right there on the seat and you want to leave. That's just the way it is, I guess."

She turned off the television. She leaned back in the chair. The tomato sauce was already beginning to stick to the pan. There was a moment in the life of a pot of ravioli, when, if you didn't rush the pan to the sink, you might as well forget it. That moment passed when Sally closed her eyes and turned sideways in the chair and draped her legs over one arm and leaned her head into the corner made by the wingback at the top of the chair.

"See, when you love somebody you can't stand to know anything bad about them. You want them to be perfect. You know they aren't. You know they can't be. But you still want them to be. Don't you see what I'm trying to tell you?" he asked. "Won't you answer me?"

She rolled out of the chair and went to the window. The snow was sticking and building up fast. An inch was on the car and on top of the trash can. A deep snow can make a person homesick, even when that person is already at home.

"You see, you get married. Later, you wonder why you did it. It's hard to figure out. It's hard to remember the way it felt, the way you both were back then. You start one way, at one place, and end up another way, in another place. So much changes. I guess you have to let it happen. I guess you have to go on."

"Let me tell you something now," she said, very slowly, as if she were controlling how she sounded. That was the first time she'd spoken in those two long days.

"I know you're trying," she said. "But you're still missing. The bad things that happen are bad, but they can be put away. Eventually you learn to treat them like bad dreams, like nightmares when you woke up and saw someone in the room and then later woke up again and nothing was there. Eventually you learn to treat them that way. You're a little scared to go to sleep, but you do.

"I'm going to tell you another story since we're into storytelling these days. I'll tell you this one and see how you like it. And then, if you want, I can tell you some more," she said.

"You see, one time we were getting ready to take a trip. Vacations were more horrible than any other time because we were all trapped in the car together. The days leading up to the vacations were as bad as the trip itself. My mother was always the one who wanted us to go. The mandatory one- or two-week family vacation every summer, just like everyone else was doing, just like all good families did. My father hated them and he'd go around for days before they began with this frozen smile on his face, a kind of grimace, a kind of hateful, vicious mask he would wear that would drive my mother absolutely crazy, so that by the time we finally left, they were both in pieces, and I was there, right in the middle of it all.

"By that time neither would be speaking to the other but we'd still go. You see. We'd still go. We had to go through the motions. If he had to ask directions and she hesitated with the map, I can see her now, trying to get it unfolded and then folded back in the right way, if she hesitated a second while he was screaming down the road about to take a wrong turn, he'd go mad, and we'd end up going the wrong way which just made the trip even longer.

"One time my mother had taken all she could. We had been on the road for two days. We were going to New England by way of Gettysburg and we stopped in Virginia and stayed in a motel. In the motels back then they had rooms with only one double bed. I slept on a cot. I didn't sleep well because I heard them talking to themselves all night, and thrashing around, pushing each other trying to get the other one to the far side of the bed and they didn't sleep well because the next day was real bad.

"We were riding along. I don't think it was on an interstate, I don't even remember interstates back then, anyway, I don't remember what kind of road it was, but we were going the speed limit, sixty-five or whatever it was, and they were fussing and fighting, and suddenly Mother opened the door and tried to jump out. My father screamed at her and grabbed her arm and held her in and yelled for me to help. The car was swerving all over the road and he was trying to get it stopped and keep her in at the same time. I reached over to grab her shoulders and pull her back but she was hanging out of the car and I couldn't reach her.

"I don't remember crying at the time, not until it was over and we had stopped and she had pulled free and run into the woods on the side of the road and Daddy and I were sitting there, in shock, I guess, watching her run up the hill.

"We had to wait a long time. I don't know how long. Then, just like that, she came back and got in the car and we started off again. Just like everything was all right. We didn't turn around. We didn't go home. We didn't go see a doctor or have her locked up or anything like that, or have us all locked up, I guess would have been the right thing. No. We just went on to Gettysburg and walked around looking at everything and I bought a doll in a soldier's uniform and a little cannon made out of brass and iron that was supposed to really shoot if you had gunpowder, and they bought some stuff, and we left, and kept on going, driving all the way to Maine, and stopping here and there at Stuckey's and places like that and buying more stuff, and we just kept on going," she said, "just kept on."

She walked out the door and onto the porch. The dog and the cat slept on a blanket. The cat rested his head on the dog's neck. They both stretched when she came out. The cold air woke her up and she stood there with the snow swirling. Robert watched her out the window. She came back a few minutes later and stood in front of him and put her hands on his shoulders, holding him, but keeping him at arm's length.

"Don't you see? It can't happen again. I can't live another life like the one I just spent so many years trying to get away from. I just can't do it. I just won't."

She walked away. She closed the bedroom door behind her. He turned on the television. It was Friday. The Dukes of Hazzard were on. Daisy was wearing short-shorts and stockings and high heels and her legs were tight and smooth and she was wearing a blouse that just wouldn't stay closed. Bo and Luke were running around acting like fools and Boss Hogg wouldn't let Roscoe have any food.

He watched the show for a few minutes. He turned it off. He hated Daisy and the promise she made with the strut and thrust of her body, the vicious female promise of everything for nothing, the promise that says, "You can have me, all you have to do is want me and hold me and be nice and then you can have me and I'll be just like you always dreamed, I'll be just like you always imagined a woman would be. Perfect, and all yours."

He hated the promise. He hated her for promising what she could not give. He hated himself for falling for it. He hated the trap of making real the unreal.

In the night, he went upstairs to bed. In the quiet of the snow and the night, he heard his wife in the room below. On a night like that, with the snow and cold outside and the sheltering house empty save the warmth of the two people in distant rooms, on a night like that, they met again.

They decided, lost and wandering in the red rage of anger, to meet again. They decided, lost and wandering in the cold blue of solitary defiance, to meet again. They decided, lost and wandering in the empty air of stubborn hatred, to meet again.

There was a stalemate. The things they feared most had

discovered where they lived. Those things moved in. Eviction would be difficult.

After the long and desperate night, at the beginning of day three, these hostages surrendered. No film recorded the act. No trained voice proclaimed the act. One had taken the other hostage and held him for ransom. One had taken the other hostage and held her for ransom. The ransom was for life.

It was, it seemed, they would later remark, a peaceful surrender and such a relief to be together again. But something was missing.

Something had been left behind. Or lost. Something like the innocence that existed before betrayal. Something like a precious object that had been carried every day from childhood and then thrown away in a sudden violent moment of unfamiliar madness, when jealousy and fear and the fresh, raw taste of revenge made their unexpected appearances.

It was, it seemed, going to be difficult to ever be the same again.

ABOUT
the AUTHOR

LAWRENCE NAUMOFF was born and raised in Charlotte, North Carolina, and graduated from the University of North Carolina, Chapel Hill. He now lives in Orange County, North Carolina.